DECISIONS

and

THE FURIES

Two Narratives of Napoleonic Times

DECISIONS
and
THE FURIES

Two Narratives of Napoleonic Times
by

MAURITS I. BOAS

FREDERICK FELL PUBLISHERS, Inc. *New York*

Library of Congress Cataloging in Publication Data

Boas, Maurits Ignatius, 1892-
   Decisions and The furies.

   1. Napoleon III, Emperor of the French, 1808-1873--
Fiction. I. Boas, Maurits Ignatius, 1892-   The
furies. 1975. II. Title.
PZ3.B63033De3 [PS3503.O125]   813'.5'2   74-28456
ISBN 0-8119-0248-X lib. bdg.

For information address:
Frederick Fell Publishers, Inc.
386 Park Avenue South
New York, N.Y. 10016

Library of Congress Catalog Card No. 74–28456

Published simultaneously in Canada by
George J. McLeod, Limited, Toronto 2B, Ontario

Manufactured in the United States of America

International Standard Book Number 0-8119-0248-x

Contents

DECISIONS

INTRODUCTION

THE GRAVEST DECISIONS, IN HISTORY AS WELL AS IN PRI-
vate life, are usually taken after long deliberation, much
soul-searching, the careful weighing of every alternative, and
in the end only after consultation with others—advisers,
friends, family perhaps. But passing over these cases in history where precautions of this sort were in fact taken, one
comes to other situations, again as in private life, where the
press of time and circumstances is so urgent that consultation is impossible, or if possible and undertaken, serves for
little, situations where the decision simply must be taken on
one's own initiative. Lessons from the past, the examples
from history or from another's experience too often seem
irrelevant, and nothing remains but to decide on the basis of

one's own best judgment, the inner voice of conscience and whatever inspiration may be afforded one.

Historical examples of such situations have been by no means rare, but few have been so brutal, so excruciating, so cruel for those involved as were those occurring during the last agonies of the Napoleonic era. Generals who had never until then been permitted the simplest independent decisions were suddenly, by force of circumstance, thrust into positions where responsibility rested on them alone, where their skill and character would determine not only the future of the nation, the throne, the safety and well-being of all Frenchmen, themselves included, but would inevitably change the whole course of history.

To the confusion of posterity the men so elected acted, with rare exceptions, in a manner contrary to what those who knew them best expected. How did it happen that men like Caulaincourt and Marmont, capable, brilliant generals, both of them, men whose worth had been proved by twenty years of service, should have acted in a fashion that could only hasten the end, in the one instance engulf Napoleon in a hopeless and useless battle and in the other force a surrender which history has regarded as shameful. The question is one the books do not answer.

Caulaincourt, a nobleman of the old school, a man incapable of the least disloyalty, of acting against his conscience or betraying the trust the Emperor had in him, was well aware at the end that a decision contrary to his commander's express wishes was the only sensible course to take, that it would work out eventually to the monarch's best interests, and yet, for all his insight and perceptiveness, he could not bring himself to make it. Why?

Marmont, one of Napoleon's closest associates, a true brother-in-arms, elevated by the Emperor to the highest rank, victor in a dozen battles, knew very well that in this crisis his benefactor's whole future, his throne and dynasty, depended on what he himself was going to do, that any advantage to be obtained at the prospective peace negotiations depended on his steadfastness and loyalty. How could it be, then, that at the moment he must decide, he should veer completely and act in the one way that would compromise everything and mean ruin for his own career?

Decisions—crucial decisions, that is—have a way of overruling the dictums of reason, have a way of being made, less on the basis of what experience advises, what cool deliberation counsels one to do, than through the impact of some more primitive force which rises from deep within the individual's consciousness.

Such, for the greater part at least, were the forces operating on Caulaincourt and Marmont, both of whom were actuated by impulses of which neither was aware, but how unpredictable the outcome of crucial decisions may be comes through even more vividly in events which occurred later when the world received news of Napoleon's sudden return. All who had been in his service, his marshals and officials, even the Bourbon-king himself, were placed in a position of having to take steps on which the remaining years of their lives would obviously depend. Either they must now join their former master in his new venture or renounce him in favor of King Louis XVIII, and in the face of this dilemma some of Napoleon's finest veterans found themselves acting in ways precisely opposite to the course which only a few days before had seemed the only reasonable one. What was it that made a Ney forget the voice of prudence, his pledged word and solemn oaths, his honor even?

A look at some of these events and the characters involved in them gives new insight into the forces that often prompt even the best-balanced and most intelligent of men to take decisions seemingly unworthy of them, decisions which seem to reflect a nature very different from the one familiar to those who feel that they know them best.

The same problem is seen again in the events which make up "The Furies". The painter Topino Lebrun, once an enthusiastic partisan of the "new ideas", now acts consistently against his own best interests. Finding himself overtaken by the past, unable to endure the memory of acts he now sees as having been crimes, he stoically accepts the fate reserved for those who find themselves hopelessly out of step with their times.

M.B.

1. CAULAINCOURT

"BELIEVE ME, CAULAINCOURT, MEN ARE DOMINATED BY only two passions. Fear and greed. These explain everything they do."

It was Napoleon speaking.

The Emperor prided himself on his ability to know men, a reputation richly deserved, if one may go by the way he chose his associates, a group of men who over the years and with few exceptions turned out to be individuals of the highest capacity, men as talented and devoted as they were brave. But even so, there is reason to wonder if, for all his intelligence, for all his perceptiveness, Napoleon wasn't more the realist than the psychologist, that is, more able to measure the exact manner in which a man might serve him than in knowing what a man might really be, what he was really worth, how he might act on his own if placed in a critical situation.

All the memoirs of the time indicate that when it came to judging men he was at heart a cynic, taking their cupidity, their unreliability, their weaknesses for granted, convinced utterly that it made no sense to expect a man to act otherwise than in accordance with his natural disposition—which, he never doubted, was bad—and that in consequence it made no sense to show grudge or bitterness toward those who did him injury. Because of this he had a reputation for magnanimity; again and again he overlooked shortcomings that no other dictator would have tolerated, but in spite of this forbearance on his part, he forever complained of being forced to delegate powers, of having no choice but to put his trust in others. Men were tools. One used them for what they were worth.

Very naturally this strictly practical approach to judging men did result in mistakes at times, mistakes which in certain instances were grave enough to do him harm, irreparable harm even, mistakes which in at least two cases not only changed the course of his life but the very course of history.

Armand de Caulaincourt and Auguste Marmont—Napoleon knew both men well. He trusted them as much as he could make himself trust anyone. Both were excellent men with long records of service and devotion; both were brave, brilliant even. Both stood so high in the opinion of the Emperor that he had ennobled them in accordance with his custom of conferring titles on those who had rendered him outstanding service; in consequence Caulaincourt was Duke of Vicenza, Marmont Duke of Ragusa. They were men who knew him well enough to act very much as he would himself when things came to a crisis. That is why on this particular day of this terrible year 1814 Napoleon never doubted he was doing the right thing when he dispatched Caulaincourt to Chatillon, there to negotiate an armistice with the allied forces who each day were pushing deeper into France. Of all the men around him, Caulaincourt was the right, the only one for that job, and in the meantime Marmont, certainly one of his most time-tested generals, could be counted on to defend the approaches of Paris to the last drop of his blood.

Caulaincourt drove off this cold February morning with an enthusiastic *"bonne chance"* from everyone. The army, the *corps diplomatique,* all who knew him agreed. Caulaincourt was a fine man, an intelligent man, considered outstanding even among that remarkable group who made up the imperial staff. He had been close to the throne for more than ten years, first as ambassador to Russia where he had been clever enough to make himself a friend of the Czar, a fact which could only work well in the present instance. Then later he was minister of foreign affairs. In this capacity he had come to know Napoleon intimately, which again was to his advantage on this mission. And there was even more that could be of help.

Caulaincourt had been born into the old nobility and as such was perfectly equipped to treat with the aristocrats of Austria, Russia, Prussia, and England. He was handsome and still in his prime, barely forty, and so well versed in the refinements of society that he could be considered "one of them." In practice, the record of his early years enabled him to stand well with both sides. As a child of the ancien regime he had entered the royal army as a lieutenant, but at the outbreak of the Revolution had embraced the new ideas, resigned his commission and privileges, and reenlisted as a private. From that point on he had climbed rapidly, as a soldier to the rank of general, as a diplomat to the high position he now held. His appointment as imperial deputy in this crucial situation only proved again how highly Napoleon esteemed him, a fact he had very much in mind today as he considered his latest responsibilities.

As he set out from imperial headquarters this fourth of February, he was grateful for the time he was going to have to think things through. Chatillon, the place of rendezvous, was a little town in the Côte d' Or of Burgundy and to reach it was going to take perhaps three days. As he was driven along over the frozen roads, doing his best to keep warm in the drafty carriage which seemed to be forever breaking down, he had only one thought: to fix in his mind the fullest possible idea of the situation he was being called upon to deal with.

One thing was plain enough—Napoleon was charging him with an almost impossible mission. The enemy was sure to be difficult, immovable in all probability. France was in a desperate position, as bad as any she had found herself in for centuries. After twenty years of victory, of conquest, the French armies had been beaten, thrown back from the Russian borders, first to Leipzig, then clear across Germany to the Rhine and over it, so that now the whole eastern region of the country and much of the north were being overrun by

Caulaincourt, Duc de Vicenza
Bibliotheque de la Ville de Paris
Collection Viollet

[17]

the combined forces of Europe. The Emperor and his few depleted corps had been forced back farther and farther, but even while giving ground he had shown the allied command that he was still the old Napoleon, the master tactician who could in an instant change defeat into victory. This campaign had been as brilliant as any he had ever fought. He had kept the army intact and dealt out a series of defeats so galling that his adversaries were at least willing to talk of peace.

Peace. Peace . . . . That was the thing most wanted by all Europe, all France, and as Caulaincourt added up the possibilities of attaining it he was glad to be able to put on the plus side the Emperor's own awareness of this developing mood among the French. At long last Napoleon seemed to be taking into account the country's war-weariness, the growing doubts, the concerns as to its leader and his place in the state. It was none too soon. Great as their admiration for their hero was, the French had suffered too much and too long and were gradually coming to see the situation without illusion. One could no longer be blind to it. The country was worn out, the army half-starved, underequipped and badly undermanned. Against 800,000 allied troops Napoleon had barely 200,000, half of them in distant theaters, all of them short of guns, horses, materiel, and if one cared to look the truth in the face, the victories of the last month had been won in most cases over isolated allied columns, leaving Blucher's Prussians in the north still free to move against the capital. Except for Marmont's scanty forces, Paris had practically no defenses at all, and—the fact was now too evident to be denied—of all this Napoleon himself was fully aware. Peace, then, almost any kind of peace, any peace that would leave France some measure of self-respect, one, say, that would guarantee France's boundaries of 1792, that was probably the most one could hope for.

Peace, yes. Even Napoleon himself favored it—at least that was what he had said. "Yes, Caulaincourt. I agree. At the moment it's the best way to capitalize on what successes we've had."

Those had been his exact words, but in his heart—and from long experience Caulaincourt had learned to sense the trend of his thoughts—he had still not abandoned his real hope, victory on the battlefield, another Austerlitz, which would place him in a position to dictate conditions rather than having to accept them. Even now, at the same moment he was sending his minister on this long excursion to Chatillon, he was marshaling his resources to continue the fight, and fighting it with all the ardor, all the ingenuity of his best days, always hoping that a major coup would make all this talk at the conference table redundant.

In the meantime, however, he had given Caulaincourt full powers, carte blanche to accept those conditions he judged to be the best obtainable. Full powers? For the tenth time Caulaincourt took out the commission and read it over. It was in the form of a letter from Maret, Napoleon's minister of state, and written only yesterday at Caulaincourt's insistence. With Napoleon one did best to be sure; it was just as well to eliminate uncertainties before they could cause difficulties. Again Caulaincourt went through the thing, going over it word by word.

> His Majesty gives you carte blanche to undertake all necessary negotiations to secure a happy conclusion, that is, the saving of the capital and the avoidance of a battle on which the last hopes of the nation would depend. It is the intention of the Emperor that you should consider yourself invested with all powers necessary to the taking of those steps which will arrest the progress of the enemy and remove the existing threat to the seat of government.

Carte blanche, full powers. A verbose piece of writing, but still unambiguous in its meaning. Very carefully he put it away. It gave him authority to proceed, treat, bargain, negotiate. Very well, then. The only question was how best to do it, how use the little bargaining power he did have. He held only one trump really, and that a purely psychological one, the enemy's fear of Napoleon, fear of his genius on the battlefield, his unbelievable daring, his proverbial good luck. This almost superstitious dread on the part of the allies, together with their desire to have done quickly with an exhausting campaign, could be enough to make them moderate their conditions and, for another thing, accept without debate Napoleon's right to continue on the throne. During these last weeks speculation as to that had been heard more and more often, a fact his Majesty still refused to take sufficiently into consideration.

Three days can be a very long time, but at last Chatillon came in sight. After so many hours on the road it was a relief to find oneself in the quarters assigned one, a handsome old house in a park on the outskirts of the town overlooking the sources of the Seine. That evening Caulaincourt met for the first time with the allied plenipotentiaries and was pleased to note that the discussions were opening amid what he took to be hopeful auguries. Count Stadion, the Austrian representative, seemed inclined to moderation—he had obviously been impressed by the fierce reaction of the Emperor's troops—and the British seemed ready to go along with him. Unfortunately the envoys of some of the smaller states showed a more hostile turn of mind, but for all that Caulaincourt did feel he could be hopeful. After two days of hard bargaining and tactful yielding on his part, signs of accommodation began to appear. The conditions proposed were certain to be regarded as very hard by the French, but all things considered, most particularly what France had inflicted on the rest of Europe, they could hardly be called excessive. What pleased him too, as yet no question as to Napoleon's retention of the throne had even been raised.

Unhappily this favorable climate soon dissipated itself. Once the talks passed from generalities to particulars, difficulties began to accumulate, and now it was the British who were the problem. Austrians, Prussians, Russians seemed ready to accept French borders based on the Rhine, the Alps and the Pyrenees, but Lord Castlereigh stated straight out that a French Antwerp would never be acceptable to England, and against this stone wall Caulaincourt's best efforts came to nothing. It left him in a harrowing position. For years now the Netherlands and Belgium had been considered an integral part of France and the surrender of France's claim to either would be regarded as a calamity. Napoleon would be outraged; almost certainly he would take out his anger on his minister, but what could one do? The plain fact was the Low Countries were already as good as lost; Holland was in open revolt and—as was now abundantly clear—

concessions, however painful, would have to be made; some flexibility on France's part must be forthcoming if the conference was to be kept going and the question of Napoleon as head of the state left out of discussion.

By the end of the first week Caulaincourt was convinced there was no other way out; he was going to have to accept the British stand; more important, he was going to have to accept it *now,* bring things to a conclusion while the allies still saw the French army as a menace and were still willing to negotiate. What made this concession all but impossible, however, were the messages that now began to arrive almost every day from the imperial headquarters. No sooner would Caulaincourt's morning report have gone forward to Napoleon than a courier would arrive with instructions to sign nothing without the Emperor's express consent; only the Emperor was able to see the situation in its entirety, and along with this came a steady volley of warnings. Holland and Belgium given up? It was an insult. Let Monsieur Caulaincourt beware these men across the table from him; guile and double dealing were second nature to them. What assurance did he have that their proposals were serious, that they really intended to make peace, that they would stop their operations when their conditions had been accepted? Weren't they merely lulling him with words while they moved their armies into ever more favorable positions?

The effect was frustrating beyond belief. Was Napoleon taking this attitude simply to delay any decision or did he really mistrust these people? Night after night Caulaincourt lay sleepless, tossing, arguing with himself what should be done, how he should proceed. France's future depended on his decision. Time was running out. Among the military, patience was wearing thin on both sides. Just this morning a messenger had arrived from Ney and two other marshals entreating him to sign, sign; the Emperor didn't realize, or didn't wish to realize, that the army was melting away, hardly more than a skeleton; in heaven's name get the thing done with!

Ney knew the facts, Ney could be trusted; no doubt existed as to that. The French position was deteriorating steadily and the bulletins which were coming in to the enemy delegations were telling the same story. Should he sign, accept the latest draft, the one submitted by Stadion? Full powers. Did he still have them? If so, he should act according to his own judgment and forget the messengers. Was not this the way to serve Napoleon's interests in the best possible fashion?

He knew Napoleon well, better perhaps than any of the others close to the great man. Of this he could be certain. Only last year he had traveled with him all the way from the Russian border back to France, most of the time the two of them alone, most of the time by sledge through hostile territory where they might have to use their pistols at any moment. Hours on end Napoleon had talked with unheard of frankness, opening a heart still smarting from the Russian disaster. Only true feelings of friendship, of trust and respect, could have motivated such confidences, and now was the moment in which to show one's self worthy of them. Fortune was giving him the opportunity to help this superman at a moment when even he needed help. It was all too plain—for once the great man had overreached himself, was blind to realities, incapable of admitting defeat even when everyone else could see the writing on the wall. Here was a chance to free him from the demons who possessed him, shield him from the effects of his own disastrous optimism, the intoxication of past glories, his mad self-confidence.

Each day and several times a day now, Caulaincourt would tell himself he must bring things to a conclusion. Napoleon had given him authority to act, had done it deliberately, knowing exactly what the consequences might be; now was the time to use this power, use it even at the risk of being raged at on his return, called a coward, a traitor. Ultimately circumstances would force the Emperor to acknowledge the correctness of his envoy's position. Wasn't the man on the ground, the man at Chatillon, the one most competent to deal with the problem? All right then. Hesitate no more. Act, and act in accordance with one's own lights. And yet—and yet, to go against the Emperor . . . he could not bring himself to do it.

Four weeks had now slipped away, the whole month of February. Napoleon's stubborn insistence that he was entitled to retain Belgium and the Netherlands, this and his continuing troop movements that threatened allied communications had dangerously embittered the tone at Chatillon. Did the Emperor of the French really consider this a peace conference, Castlereigh wanted to know, or was he merely using it as another Prague or Frankfort where negotiations were broken off the moment the French military situation improved sufficiently? Unrest had come to a crisis point among the delegates; some were for breaking off discussions then and there, others for forcing Caulaincourt

[24]

to accept the offered terms, but in spite of these dissentions among themselves the allies did come to agreement on one point, the very one Caulaincourt had most feared. On March 9th they signed a joint declaration saying there could be no peace with Napoleon. To treat with the man was an impossibility, and they would do so no longer.

For Caulaincourt this was the finishing blow. It left him powerless. Each time he tried to argue the point that Napoleon was head of government in France, and that other than treating with him no means for coming to an understanding with the French did in fact exist, the plenipotentiaries threatened to declare the proceedings closed. From that point on the meetings were little more than forums in which the allies accused Napoleon—not implausibly—of using Chatillon as a ruse to win time to reinforce his army, precisely the kind of double dealing he had a few days before been imputing to them. It could hardly have come as a surprise then that around the middle of March they should announce, unilaterally, that the congress did stand adjourned. From now on they would devote themselves to a military solution, since that was the one Napoleon obviously preferred.

Very early in the morning of March 21st Caulaincourt left Chatillon. He was a bitter man. What had his so-called commission amounted to? An elaborate fraud, a fraud first to last. Napoleon had sent him up a blind alley. Each time he had tried to act the Emperor had thrust a spoke in the wheel, and now it was too late. But what about France? The agonizing question was, what was going to happen to France? What was to be done about that? What was his own personal contribution going to be?

[25]

On his way back to the imperial lines he was escorted as far as Joigny by an Austrian colonel, and then, after a day wasted following false leads, he finally came up with the Emperor on March 24th at Saint-Dizier in French-held territory.

Napoleon was beside himself. Hadn't he said it all along? The allies had been making fools of them. Look at Blucher. He'd cashed in on all this palavering by pushing the 6th Corps back on Paris, and here at Saint-Dizier the main body of the Austrians had managed to disengage. Chatillon? From the first he had known what those bandits were up to. Action. Action. That was the only thing they respected, the only thing they feared. Suppose the rain *had* turned the roads into swamps, suppose the troops *were* exhausted. "We must get at them, beat them before it's too late!" And turning to Caulaincourt, "You let them make a fool of you!" he said. "They never did want peace. The only thing they were after was the chance to put more tarnish on the honor of old France . . ."

Caulaincourt came back at him. Peace could have been had. Peace could be had even now, and somehow, some way, they *must* get back to the conference table again. He argued and argued and managed to hold the Emperor's ear far into the night, but nothing came of it. Each of Caulaincourt's points, the state of the troops, the inexperience of the new formations, the discouragement caused by the failure at Chatillon, was rejected in turn. Still Caulaincourt, whose ego had been left in shreds, refused to let himself be silenced. France could be saved, even Napoleon's throne could be saved. But it was no use. Each time he found himself rebuffed, but each time he returned to the charge, and for the five days he remained with Napoleon at this stage it went on like this, with Napoleon making fun of him for his credulity and at the same time praising him for having refused to make a dishonorable peace.

"It would have been a disgrace," he told him, and with that supremely self-certain smile of his he added, "We'll make a victory out of this yet, Caulaincourt. You'll see!"

In the meantime, with each passing day, the news became more alarming. It was apparent now that Napoleon had been outmaneuvered. In taking his main body west as far as Troyes he had been expecting to draw Schwarzenberg's Austrians after him at which point the two corps commanded by Macdonald and Oudinot would swing around and cut the enemy's communications. Instead, he now found that those Austrians who had followed him were no more than a corps of observation while Schwarzenberg's main strength had bypassed him and was moving directly on Paris. Latest reports indicated they had already passed through Meaux and were mounting their siege guns on the hills just outside the capital. Meanwhile the 6th Corps facing Blucher had itself fared badly. After being pushed back again and again it had at the last minute drawn off to a position south of Paris halfway between that city and Fontainebleau.

Once the threat to Paris became clear, Napoleon ordered all his troops to concentrate. The capital must be defended. There was not a moment to lose. Those farthest distant would have four days to make the march and not a minute longer. With that, he himself and the Guard began the long race back.

That same day, as the Emperor and his staff moved along the rain-drenched roads toward Paris, a dispatch rider met them just beyond Fontainebleau. Appalling news. Paris had capitulated already. This, coming on top of the tactical setback just sustained, was more than even a Napoleon could take. Caulaincourt could not recall having ever seen him in such a condition, not even on the days along the Berezina. Let his carriage be readied! He would drive on, straight to Paris, show himself to the people, rally the National Guard, drive the invaders out!

It was only at great pains that Caulaincourt and Berthier were able to dissuade him. The gates of Paris would already be manned by the enemy; the Emperor would only be risking capture. Giving in at last, Napoleon turned back to Fontainebleau. For the time being imperial headquarters would be established there, and only then, after twenty-four hours without sleep, did he let himself be persuaded to take some rest.

Here at last Caulaincourt had a chance to get some idea of the situation as it really was. An inspection of the troops on the ground showed that their numbers had shrunk frightfully, partly through casualties and sickness, partly through desertion. As for the military possibilities, what point was there in denying it? They had changed radically and for the worse. In trying to lure the enemy west, Napoleon had thrown away precious time and the surrender of Paris looked to be the consequence. But to hear Napoleon tell it, he need only complete the concentration of his troops, join Marmont and the 6th Corps at Essonne, and strike the enemy rear, strike hard, and everything would be retrieved.

The men around the Emperor were stunned. Could he really be so blind to the realities, to his lack of means to deal with the enormous mass of the enemy, to the peril he himself was in with Blucher to the north and the Austrians and Bavarians lapping around him to the east? Couldn't he see that any attack such as he envisaged was not merely reckless, but close to suicidal? Only a miracle could bring it off, but then, they reflected, miracles had never been strangers to Napoleon, and perhaps here again a miracle might be conceivable, not one for the military, to be sure, but one for the diplomats. The news leaking through from Paris showed the allies' fears of the Napoleonic strategy were still as real as ever and even seemed to be growing as they watched the Emperor pull his forces together. The odds for a diplomatic success might not be what they had been at Chatillon, but there was still a chance that with proper handling negotiations could lead to some tolerable solution. They must do their best to make this clear to his imperial Majesty.

In plain truth, though he would never have admitted it, Napoleon was quite aware how slender his possibilities were, quite aware too that the conclusion of an armistice, no matter how disadvantageous, offered him the best and perhaps the only chance to save his throne. That thoughts like these might be going through his head was something no one could have even guessed, but late that evening he summoned Caulaincourt. He had decided to send him off again, this time to Paris. He must find out just what the possibilities for peace really were—Napoleon walked the room—but it would have to be done very adroitly.

"Get in touch with the Czar and Schwarzenberg. Make

yourself agreeable any way you can, talk as if we were ready for any kind of settlement, but . . ." Napoleon reached up and pinched his visitor's ear, "put in a word about Marmont." The pacing began again. "Tell them how close he is to Paris, how easily the 6th Corps can move on the city or strike the Austrian flank. Say something about the Guard being here with me. They know the Guard. And they know Marmont and what he can do. Stir their fears, flatter their hopes, one way or another keep them busy until I've had time to get my men together."

Caulaincourt had to smile. Very plainly Napoleon was still what he had always been, the master tactician, as much at the conference table as in the field.

"Get some rest now." Napoleon went to the door. "And be off in the morning. Early."

There was much grumbling that night among the marshals. Caulaincourt? Caulaincourt again? It was not envy. Not one of them would have cared to be in Caulaincourt's shoes; they simply doubted the Emperor's wisdom in banking so strongly on him. What had the man been able to accomplish at Chatillon? He had known all along that the country's destiny was in his hands, and what had he come up with? Things standing as they did now, the situation being as desperate as it was, what right had one to expect wonders from this fine gentleman, this one-time marquis?

That last set them all talking. They had never thought much about it before, the kind of man Caulaincourt really was. There wasn't much you could say against him. They all admitted it: Caulaincourt was a very likable man; a decent man, clever, conscientious, and a lot more, but—for all that —how should one put it, he was not a man like themselves, unprejudiced, practical in his outlook, in the way he thought and acted. Tradition, that was the trouble. The man was too steeped in tradition. One look at his past, his background, told the whole thing. His father? A general and the son of a general, the complete gentleman of the old school, full of ideas about honor and rectitude, and his son—why, naturally, his son had followed in his father's footsteps. Brought up in that right-thinking, right-acting world where obedience was not only a duty but a matter of honor, he had done what his father had done, seen his duty in exactly the same way the latter had when he decided he must embrace the Revolution. Since then Caulaincourt had done his best to make himself a good democrat and, God knows, he had, for the greater part anyway, but . . . even so, one look at the man was enough to tell you he never had been, and never would be, able to make himself a true son of the people.

Indeed, it *was* this, this very tradition of fidelity and rectitude, which accounted for his failure at Chatillon. Caulaincourt had simply found it impossible *not* to be the gentleman. He had continued to be the gentleman even when circumstance demanded he forget his code, forget honor and morality for the moment, forget the respect and obedience a soldier owes his superior. But how had it worked out, this devotion to being a gentleman, at other times in his life, in the rough-and-tumble of the world? How had it worked out in his other dealings with Napoleon when his own private interests had been involved, to take just one example, that day he had told Napoleon he wanted to marry?

[31]

That story dated back quite a number of years. His love had been an unhappily married woman abandoned by her husband and eager for the divorce that would have let her marry Caulaincourt. Yet, when Napoleon was asked for his consent, consent was refused. The word divorce was out of favor with the great man since his own divorce was then in prospect, and Caulaincourt submitted. Nevertheless he continued to attend the lady for almost ten years, and only this last summer, with the imperial consent finally granted, in part at least as a reward for services rendered in the most difficult of times, had the marriage taken place. It was clear enough that in this instance too Caulaincourt had been unable to go against the rules, to act in a way that might even faintly resemble insubordination, that worst of all sins.

One of the marshals came up with a comparison between his attitude at Chatillon and that of Count von Haugwitz, the Austrian representative, at the Pressburg conference, Haugwitz who for all his lack of full powers had nevertheless signed the treaty for Austria knowing full well that in so doing he was acting in contravention of his monarch's expressed wishes. Haugwitz, it was pointed out, had acted in that fashion because he was certain in his own mind that to sign, and sign immediately, was the only intelligent thing to do. But Caulaincourt at Chatillon? Not at all. Loyalty had been his only maxim and at a moment when loyalty was undoubtedly the virtue least to be desired.

Another of the marshals then wondered what Talleyrand might have done had he been the man at Chatillon. Talleyrand? A chuckle ran around the room. Talleyrand would never have bothered to think twice of duty or loyalty when the national interest, or his own for that matter, happened to be at stake. What difference would it have made to Talleyrand, some loss of face, some hard words from the imperial lips, even a few unpleasant adjectives perhaps in the history books of years to come?

Caulaincourt knew only too well what his colleagues had been thinking. They hadn't been able to mask their feelings, and that afternoon of March 31st, when he finally did get off to Paris, he couldn't help asking himself if in fact there had been something wanting in his performance. However that might be, he would be thinking this time of France only, the French case, France's predicament and how best to help her, forgetting himself and—all the rest of that. First of all he must never lose sight of the military realities—an army perilously scattered, troops here, troops there, the Lyon contingent too far off to even be taken into consideration, and Marmont's corps, intact but weak and outnumbered, down to less then 12,000 effectives, some said. It was going to be hard, more than hard, to put up that confident front Napoleon had demanded. It would be hard, but he still felt if success was possible at all, he was the one man most likely to achieve it.

News reaching his ears the moment he entered Paris was little apt to lessen his concerns. Not only was the whole city in the hands of the enemy but talk in the streets was only of the mistakes of the imperial regime and the need for a return to normal, which in practical terms meant the return of the Bourbons. The Empress, apparently, along with her four-year-old son and many members of the government had left the city at the last minute for Rambouillet, leaving Joseph Bonaparte, inept as usual, in full charge as governor of Paris. Joseph, inevitably, decided within the hour that he'd do better to forget all thought of defense and save Paris from bombardment by surrendering the city. This in turn provoked a wave of disloyalty, of rebellion even. The Senate, or what was left of the Senate, immediately rallied to Talleyrand, declared Napoleon dethroned, and then proceeded to reorganize itself as a provisional government.

These events had succeeded each other with such rapidity that Caulaincourt realized that if he was to accomplish anything it would have to be now. As soon as he could find out where the Czar had established headquarters—it turned out to be at a chateau on the eastern outskirts—he hurried there and presented himself. They did not make him wait. To his relief, too, he was received without ceremony and with the kindest of words as if he and his Majesty had parted only yesterday. "The Duke of Vicenza is the kind of friend one is always happy to welcome," and Alexander added that once he was able to occupy his quarters in town—they were to be in M. Talleyrand's house, rue St. Florentin—"M. Caulaincourt must feel free to come and see me there at any time." Meanwhile a passport was being readied which would permit the Duke to move about the city as freely as he might wish.

It was all very cordial, but as soon as he touched on the business in hand, especially on the possibility of reopening negotiations, the Czar made his position very clear.

"No, no, my friend. Put that out of your head. There can be no peace with Napoleon, we are all agreed on that. So long as that man remains at large Europe can never breathe freely."

This he repeated over and over again. Nothing Caulaincourt could say could make him change it, and yet, in spite of the categorical tone, he could sense, from certain remarks, certain questions, questions asked as if in passing about the Old Guard and its whereabouts, "that wonderful body of fighting men," that underneath the show of implacability the old fear still lingered. Along with this went a noticeable uncertainty about the French themselves, the Parisians particularly, their temper, their unpredictability. Taken together it left a glimmer of hope that some arrangement was still possible, the sort of arrangement which would preserve the dynasty, at least in the form of a Regency for Napoleon's son. To Caulaincourt's surprise, the Czar seemed to see nothing out of place in such a solution, which in itself was so encouraging it almost seemed a positive success.

After that came a visit to Schwarzenberg, but the Field-marshal was icy. If it was peace Napoleon wanted, he could have had it at Chatillon. Why talk of it now? Try as he might, Caulaincourt could not sway him, and after a few last inconsequential exchanges there was nothing to do but bow himself out. Here too Napoleon's departure seemed the prerequisite for any discussion of peace, and the question of a Regency hadn't even been allowed to come up.

Peace, then. But with whom was it to be negotiated? What of the French themselves, what were they thinking?

Back in the city, he went straight to Talleyrand. At his palatial house he was told the Prince was in conference, busy, very busy, but after a minute the would-be head of state did come out and meet him in an anteroom. Apparently he was astonished to discover Caulaincourt was in Paris.

"The Emperor has ruined us all," he said, looking his visitor in the eyes. "He should have let you make peace at Chatillon," and the expression on his face, half-inquiring, half-sarcastic, seemed to ask, "Why in heaven's name didn't you?"

It was this failure, Talleyrand argued, to make peace while peace was possible, that had destroyed Napoleon's credit with the French people, left them no choice but to make sure of their future as best they could. That was only sensible, was it not? So why keep on talking about Napoleon? Napoleon was finished. And from that point on the discussion took on such a tone of bitterness that Caulaincourt was relieved when the arrival of two members of Talleyrand's "government" cut short the interview. It was plain the Prince and he were no longer speaking the same language.

After spending what was left of the night at his sister's house, Caulaincourt was off early to pay another call on the Czar. The question was, would a representative of the Regency, if a Regency were in fact established, be received as an accredited representative by the allies? But no direct answer as to this was forthcoming even though the idea itself was not categorically rejected. The situation being what it was, this offered some hope as a basis to build on.

These hopes were quickly dampened at his next stop, the chamber of the Senate. The Senate, it was plain, had had done with the Empire, a fact that was hardly surprising if one recalled that most of the members had compromised themselves already by declaring for the Bourbons. With a

Napoleon on the throne, or even near the throne, their lives could scarcely be considered safe, and in addition it was more than clear that the members' chief concern, first, last and all the time, was to maintain themselves in office. With them any suggestion that the Bonapartes might stay on was plainly doomed in advance.

Unfortunate as this was, the opinion of the Senators, individually or collectively, would never be of major importance in influencing the events about to take place. Talleyrand, though, was of a very different caliber, in this situation a really dangerous man, and such being the case Caulaincourt decided he must make one more call on him before starting back to Fontainebleau. He was hoping to get a little better idea of what the man was actually up to, but the visit almost ended in blows.

A number of other personalities were present at this meeting, among them Pradt, Napoleon's one-time ambassador at Warsaw, and the words Pradt now used to vent his wrath on Napoleon were so extreme that Caulaincourt finally lost his temper. Taking the man by the lapels, he began to shake him. This miserable self-seeker, so outspoken now where once he had been so mouselike, this unspeakable hypocrite —he was no better than a scoundrel. They were finally separated by several highly excited dignitaries.

Up to a point these emotions were understandable enough. For all of these men the consequences of his even being in Paris constituted a mortal threat, and that Talleyrand himself was fully aware of this was very easy to see. It would in fact be his chief reason for doing everything he could to eliminate the thought of Napoleon continuing on as Em-

[37]

peror from the minds of the Parisians. He might not be ready yet to dismiss the possibility of a Regency out of hand, but he did make it sufficiently clear that he had no great enthusiasm for the idea.

By the time he left the rue St. Florentin Caulaincourt would have had to admit that, even if goodwill on all sides could be restored, the practical difficulties of setting up such a government would be enormous. Who, for example, would hold power during the minority of Napoleon's son? Certainly not Napoleon. The Czar had made that absolutely clear; Napoleon's presence in France would no longer be tolerated, and as far as the "titan's" future was concerned, the real problem was to find some decent place of exile for him, Russia, Austria, Corfu, Elba. As for Regent, the Czar had hinted strongly that the only name acceptable to the allies would be that of the Empress Marie Louise.

In spite of the ill-will of Talleyrand and his crowd, this last did mean that Caulaincourt on his return to Fontainebleau could give his master some small measure of encouragement. The picture was somber, but not necessarily hopeless. In view of the Czar's moderation there was a real possibility that the dynasty itself might still be saved, and he explained that in detail to Napoleon.

However, here at Fontainebleau things had been happening too, serious things. It took only the first words of his colleagues to show that the mood of the army had radically changed. Oudinot's corps had come in just that morning and the marshal made no secret of the temper of his men. The long march had been too much for them and once they heard talk of one last battle under the walls of Paris the grumbling had begun. Another battle now was more than they would take, even for Napoleon. Macdonald, another of Napoleon's best fighting generals, had the same tale to tell. His command had arrived the night before and was as disaffected as Oudinot's, while Marmont who had been at Fontainebleau this last afternoon had had a lot to say too about low morale among his men at Essonne.

That evening, the marshals had Caulaincourt in to meet with them. It was their opinion a stand had to be taken; things couldn't go on as they were and it was time they made this clear. As a result, next morning a delegation that included eight marshals headed by Ney waited on the Emperor and told him straight out that the men in the ranks were in no condition to endure even one more day of combat. Macdonald put it even more bluntly. The men in his corps had had it; very simply, they would fight no longer.

"They will if I ask them to," Napoleon countered.

"No, Sire, they will not," Ney broke in. "They will obey their generals."

Macdonald backed this by giving a long account of the state of his troops, the toll taken these last three months, their discouragement, their complete exhaustion. Desertions, once unheard of, were increasing now each passing day. Batallions were not batallions anymore; they were remnants scraped together from as many as a dozen regiments. The time had come when the truth had to be faced.

Napoleon listened and said nothing.

In years past, a confrontation such as this would have brought on an outburst, a scene of violence with threats of arrest, court-martial, degradation, but this time there was

[39]

none of it. He paced the room, hands clasped behind his back. After a minute he turned, his face a mask, and declared that if it appeared he was the one obstacle to peace he was willing to step down; he would do whatever was necessary for the good of the country and would consent to the terms of a peace negotiated on that basis. To make it clear that such was his intention, he was sending Caulaincourt into Paris again, this time with a letter to the Czar which would state that if no other way existed to give Europe peace, the Emperor of the French was ready to abdicate in favor of his son.

Silence followed, but after another interval of pacing he added that to give weight to the delegation he would also be sending Ney and Macdonald along, and with that and without adding another word, he dismissed them. Within the hour the letter to the Czar had been written, signed and handed to Caulaincourt along with a letter addressed to him personally in which he was again granted full powers to conclude a settlement and with the further assurance that this time the terms, no matter what, would be ratified without alteration.

2. MARMONT

EARLY NEXT MORNING, APRIL FOURTH, WITH THE CAR-
RIAGES already waiting, word came that the Emperor must
see his deputies once more. He had a few more instructions
to give; first, that they do their best to incline the Czar
toward a policy of consideration for the Paris population;
further, that they make it clear, clear to all, that the French
army was still undefeated and had now completed its concentration.

His tone and his manner left them with the strong impression that he was still not persuaded the end had come, that
even now his plans called for one final appeal to the fortunes
of war. It was not that he ever said this in so many words,
but the way he first outlined the situation and then issued his

orders suggested he was still thinking primarily in military terms. As an instance, he made a point of instructing them to see Marmont in passing. They must repeat his orders that Essonne must be held *at any cost,* and turning to Caulaincourt, he added: "I'm lucky to have Marmont in command of the VIth; Marmont understands the strategic importance of his position." This seemed to carry the same implications.

At length Napoleon released them. Thanks to good weather, they were at Essonne in less than two hours and saw Marmont immediately. As Marmont heard them outline their mission—the negotiation of a peace based on a Regency, this to be accomplished through the implied threat of Napoleon's continuing the fight—a certain embarrassment began to be noticeable in him, an embarrassment which also showed in the faces of those of his staff who were in the room. It was as if there was something Marmont would prefer not to talk about, and only when he heard them say they were going directly to the Czar did he draw Macdonald aside and tell him in a half whisper that he himself was in touch with the allied command, that in fact he had already started negotiations.

Appalled, Macdonald turned to the others and repeated what he had just heard, and Marmont, seeing how stunned they were, started to explain, deliberately at first, then with growing emotion.

"Don't hold it against me. Think how it's been, Paris ready to quit, surrender without even fighting. This man of Talleyrand, they sent him to tell me they'd already voted out Napoleon, that I was to get the *troupes de ligne* out of town, Talleyrand was heading the new provisional government, and it was up to me to sign the necessary orders. Put yourself in my place! What was I to do?" There was a helpless gesture. "Joseph had already signed the surrender. The Prussians were already in the town . . ." And when there was still no word from any of them, his tone became almost pleading. "You know as well as I do. We have no chance. France is beaten, but that man is ready to have us all die, right here. I had to do whatever I could to see that didn't happen."

Caulaincourt recovered first.

"But what *have* you done? What exactly have you done?"

"Well . . . " There was a long pause. "I went to see Schwarzenberg. He insisted I sign the Paris surrender terms too, and after I'd done that he accepted my offer to . . . to . . ."

"Your offer?"

"Yes . . ." And after another hesitation he went on in an almost inaudible voice, "My offer to march my troops to Normandy."

"Normandy!" There was a dead silence.

Then someone asked, "When did this happen?"

Another helpless shrug. "I could see no other way. It was last night. Two o'clock this morning, to be exact."

The marshals stared at each other. Then Caulaincourt burst out:

"You've taken away our last chance for decent terms! Our only hope was their fear, fear of a French army with Napoleon heading it! What argument do we have if that army no longer exists!"

Apparently this got home with Marmont. All at once he seemed to realize how things stood, that there might still have been a chance. Too late the awareness was coming of the fatal consequences of the step he had taken. Mumbling to himself, he walked to the far end of the room while the others stood silent.

At last Caulaincourt got hold of himself. "Has anything been signed?"

"No. Nothing. Not about that."

"Well—in that case nothing's been done that can't be undone. If you haven't signed, the thing's not binding."

Marmont nodded. Yes, he agreed, that was true. He supposed he could annul the whole thing, and he would just as soon do it, tell Schwarzenberg he had changed his mind.

"Good," Ney broke in. "Here." He snatched up a piece of paper and thrust it down on the table. "Sit down and write it out for him."

Marmont sat as he was told, but confronted by the blank sheet seemed to hesitate. He appeared defeated by the prospect of having to spell out such a thing in black and white, and his manner as he stared ahead, holding the pen in his hand but writing nothing, brought new misgivings to the watchers. Caulaincourt cut this short.

"Well, if you can't bring yourself to write it, come with us. You can tell him face to face!"

At the moment this must have seemed the easier way. Marmont got up, visibly relieved. All right, he'd join them, but even before they were through the door he was holding them back. Apparently he felt he still had some explaining to do.

"It struck me I was doing the right thing. As I saw it, it was in my power to save the Emperor from capture, and even more, prevent civil war, because that's what will happen if

Le Duc de R.....

Marmont, Duc de Raguse
Litho d'apres Leclerc
Collection Viollet

[45]

he goes on fighting. Fighting? It would be a guerrilla war, ruin for the country. But the Emperor? We all know him. He'd sacrifice everything, men, country, to avoid the kind of peace the rest of us know is inevitable," and turning from one to the other, "Facts! Look at the facts! Cossacks everywhere, pillaging, burning, raping. It struck me Talleyrand was right. I thought I was serving my country as a good patriot."

Caulaincourt's only response was to repeat the Emperor's latest order: under no circumstance was the VIth Corps to move from where it was now. "Is that understood?"

"But of course. That's understood."

"Fine. Then let's be going."

The man with the laisser-passer had just come in. They had to have it to be admitted to the enemy lines, but as they stepped outside and were waiting for the carriages to be brought around, Marmont drew Caulaincourt aside and in a rather unsteady voice asked him what he thought the Emperor was apt to think about all this.

"Think? There's only one way to handle that. Once we've finished our business in Paris go straight to Fontainebleau and tell him everything."

This evoked nothing, and from the way he received the advice Caulaincourt could guess Marmont would almost certainly not follow it; possibly he was even seeing it as part of a maneuver to get him into custody. Head down, he stepped into the carriage, and all the way to Paris hardly opened his mouth.

In Paris they parted, with Caulaincourt going straight to the Czar. Though by this time it was two in the morning, he was admitted promptly and once again received in the

[46]

friendliest fashion. It took only the first few words to make it evident the Czar knew all about Marmont's agreement of the night before, and when Caulaincourt told him that Marmont had now changed his mind, that he was rescinding the whole thing and the allies must be prepared to fight, Alexander reacted with surprise and disbelief which turned very shortly into anger. It was pointless to continue the discussion. He wouldn't have another thing to say until his allies had had word of this turnabout.

Left with no other choice, Caulaincourt put the rest of his business over to next day. He needed rest badly. His companions and he were spending the night each in his own house, but before they parted it had been decided that they would all meet in the morning at Ney's, breakfast at half past eleven.

Well before that time Caulaincourt had had a chance to see various people. Evidently word of Marmont's latest change of heart had already got about, and the mere fact that he had come into Paris with Caulaincourt and apparently made up part of Napoleon's delegation, was taken as proof that the story was correct. It was enough to send chills along the spines of the provisional government, and Caulaincourt was bombarded with questions. What was it all about, what were they trying to get for Napoleon anyway? A Regency? Ridiculous! France wouldn't hear of it. Talleyrand was indignant. Though Talleyrand could usually be counted on to come up with an epigram, the best thing he could offer this time was scorn. Napoleon would always be there, wouldn't he, "eavesdropping" in the background. A Regency could only be a disaster.

[47]

Marechal Mortier, Duc de Trevise
After Lariviere, Musee de Versailles
Collection Viollet

The mood in the allied camp was hardly less taut. With Marmont slipping away, their spirits sank. As long as he stood there with the others, firm under the imperial eagles, their problem was still with them.

At exactly eleven thirty Caulaincourt arrived at Ney's. Macdonald had got there a few minutes earlier, but as yet no Marmont. They waited—fifteen minutes, a half hour, and when they finally sat down and ate there was very little talk. The mood was somber; they recalled how silent he had been when he parted with them the night before, and now where was he, what would he be up to?

Just as they were getting up from table the missing one made his appearance. He had been to see Schwarzenberg, he told them, and had given notice he was breaking off all contacts and would be joining his colleagues in going to see the Czar, but then minutes later, and even before Marmont had had time to finish his coffee, an officer of the VIth Corps staff, a certain Colonel Fabvier, was ushered in. He would like a word in private with his chief. The man's tenseness, the expression on his white, cramped face, was enough to upset the others all over again. They sat there silent, filled with forebodings, waiting for Marmont to return.

When he did reappear he was in a terrible state, hardly able to speak.

"I've been disgraced, disgraced forever," he gasped, and slumped into a chair. "I'm lost! lost!"

The others waited. What had happened came out haltingly. Fabvier had told him that during the past night the greater part of the VIth Corps, on orders of certain of its generals, had moved into the Austrian lines and taken up the positions originally agreed upon in the tentative agreement with Schwarzenberg. Apparently a messenger from Napoleon had arrived, ordering these men to report to Fontainebleau, and fearing the Emperor's wrath if he learned of their contacts with Schwarzenberg they had decided to take responsibility for this step themselves.

"I'd give my right arm to undo it!" Marmont wailed.

Ney glared at him. "Why not your head?"

For a time nothing more was said. Each was trying to visualize what this meant—finis to their efforts to win acceptable terms, finis to their efforts to preserve the Napoleonic dynasty. A Regency? All chance for that was now definitely gone.

This became even clearer moments after they were admitted to see the Czar. Apparently he had been informed of everything, and his attitude was stern. Napoleon had to go, he and all his family. Only if his guests were willing to accept that point as settled could he treat with them further. And even then it might be better to let the whole matter rest until they'd heard what the King of Prussia and Prince Schwarzenberg had to say.

For Caulaincourt and his two fellow deputies nothing remained now but to return to Fontainebleau for new instructions. Their only real chance had rested on the existence of an effective army, and the defection of the VIth Corps marked the army's final disintegration.

Napoleon's response to the news was so bitter that for a time it seemed he was forgetting what all this meant for him personally.

A Caricature of Marmont's attitude shortly before Napoleon's fall. "Geusar" is Raguse with letters reversed

Collection Viollet

[51]

"Marmont! That Marmont should do this to me! Marmont, my oldest friend, the one I trusted most!"

He paced the room. "I made him, I stood by him always, I believed in him, I believed in his integrity. He's been with me from the first, grew up in my camp, fed at my table, married by my arrangement. I loaded him with honors, honors and wealth. But that's how it goes—the ones I've raised the highest are the first to abandon me. Why? What makes them? Ambition! Conceit! He's hoping to take credit for saving Paris, for being the savior of France!"

The Emperor would have done well to spare at least one of his commanders in this indictment. Mortier's division of the VIth was still standing firm at Essonne. Mortier had been approached by Talleyrand with the same arguments that had persuaded Marmont, but Mortier had refused even to listen. There had not been a moment's hesitation with him, and his troops stood back of him to a man.

As for Marmont, chance had taken the climactic decision out of his hands, but he was still faced with one difficult moment. Next morning when his troops realized where they were, surrounded, helpless, they got completely out of hand. At the risk of his life Marmont faced them, and with an adroit harangue succeeded in calming them down. The damage had been done, and since there was no way of reversing it, why complicate the situation by making trouble now, and in the end the men stacked their arms and accepted the *fait accompli.*

With that, all formal resistance by the French was at an end. All that remained were formalities, formalities which imposed very hard conditions on France and sent Napoleon into exile.

For both Caulaincourt and Marmont the story would have an epilogue, however. After April 6th, the day the Emperor did what he had to do—signed the letter of abdication both for himself and his son and agreed to retirement in Elba—Marmont was the focus of universal attention. Having faced down his rebellious army, he had now to face down public opinion, and from the first it was evident it would be no easy task. Already the verdict was coming in against the man whose stupefying act had brought down the giant. Even while the final negotiations were in progress, it became clear that for the nation Marmont, Duke of Ragusa, was a marked man. All during the next generation he would remain the most unpopular man in France, and even the honors which the Bourbons on their return showered upon him could not shield him from this universal rejection.

Within weeks *raguser* was a byword meaning to betray, and Ragusa a term carrying with it all the implications the name Quisling would have in a later age. When in 1830, as Governor of Paris, he led the royal troops in the street fighting of the July Revolution he barely escaped lynching and only saved his life by fleeing to the Rhine in a hired carriage. It was an exile from which he would never return. There would be a few months in Vienna as one hired by Metternich to instruct the young Duke of Reichstadt in the history of his father's campaigns, but for the most part he would keep to North Italy visiting the old battlefields. There, in Venice, he would die in 1854, a forgotten man.

ENIGMATIC DECISIONS

WHAT WAS IT, THOUGH, THAT WOULD INCITE A MAN AS respected, as brilliant and reputable as Marmont to cast himself so suddenly and quite unnecessarily in the Judas role? For years Marmont would be the subject of argumentation, a topic as intriguing as "the Caulaincourt case" might have been had its details been more widely known. Friends and colleagues did their best to do him justice, to understand the psychology of this man they had thought they knew so well, and who so unexpectedly had acted in a way that set him apart from everything he had stood for in the past. Had Napoleon been right in his final assessment? Had it been greed, fear, petty selfishness that impelled him? No. No indeed. Those who knew him best refused to see it that way.

In no instance before had Marmont ever shown one single sign of disloyalty or unreliability. On the contrary, he had always been, as the Emperor had pointed out repeatedly, one he could count on, one to be trusted in any situation, a man brave in battle, blessed with initiative and ready to sacrifice himself if sacrifice was called for. They recalled his superior conduct on various occasions. It was he who had taken responsibility in 1800 for transporting the artillery across the St. Bernard. It was he who that year at Marengo had turned defeat into victory with the support of Kellerman's cavalry. During the time he was governor of Dalmatia he had distinguished himself in yet another field, building roads, public works, reorganizing the administration, with a show of talent which had impressed even Napoleon. One might say that each step in his career up to the fatal day at Essonne had shown him to be a man whose instinct was to act for the good of all, and if it happened that along the way he had acquired wealth, titles and honors, it was due to recognition by the Emperor of work well done and not to pride, avarice, or other flaw of character.

In other words, any theory which asserts that his defection was undertaken primarily to protect his rank and possessions will hardly hold. Considerations of this sort may possibly have played some part in the backwaters of his mind, but in view of the uncertainties as to what might follow, as to what the political developments in France might be, such a motivation could hardly have been predominant. In the end many of his critics simply gave up—for one reason or another he had turned out to be a traitor; quite evidently, they had never really known the man at all.

[56]

Certain details have come to light which only complicate the mystery. One often cited is a note written by a certain Laffitte and forwarded to Marmont during the worst days of 1814. In it Lafitte begs a mutual friend to approach the marshal and plead the uselessness of further resistance. But how much effect would such appeals have had on the man? Up to a point they may have had some influence, but they can hardly have been persuasive enough to account for the tragic thing that actually did happen.

It is not in documents like these but in Marmont's own past that one should look for the really decisive clues. First, one should note that for all his loyalty to Napoleon there are signs of occasional disagreements, of a latent envy, old and deep, that goes back to the earliest days of their association. They had been schoolmates together, Marmont and Bonaparte; Marmont had been a good comrade to the then threadbare young Corsican who was only too glad to get himself a square meal in the house of his friends, the Marmont family. They had entered the royal artillery together, served side by side at Toulon, marched together in Egypt; and though Marmont had been steadily advanced in rank and awarded honor after honor, it must have been hard at times to watch his old-time classmate climb to heights which completely overshadowed him.

This sort of never-acknowledged rivalry would show itself in various facets of Marmont's private life. When during the Spanish campaign he replaced Marshal Massena and found himself for the first time heading a completely independent command, almost his first move was to create around him a scene of near-princely luxury.

[57]

"In Valladolid," General Thiebault writes, "he set up a household matching that of a sovereign, with brilliant receptions, hour-long meals, magnificent balls, two hundred servants in red livery supervised by twelve majordomos, three intendants, etc., etc. To meet the need of this train cost as much as to feed a whole regiment." In place of the Mameluk Napoleon had brought back with him from Egypt, Marmont kept at his heels a giant Dalmatian decked out in the brightest colors.

Once he had tasted life on this exalted scale it must have been harder than ever to take the not-too-flattering language Napoleon was so prone to use in moments of displeasure. Over the next few years, as things went from bad to worse, Marmont would find himself again and again on the receiving end of dressing-downs couched in the roughest terms, and in the March days just preceding his capitulation there had been words that cut like a lash, words like those which followed the battle of Laon in which Napoleon accused Marmont of conducting himself like a sublieutenant. Again, in a letter dated March 4th to Clarke, the war minister, a letter which came under the eyes of many, Napoleon scoffed at Marmont's "insufferable vanity." "He is always misunderstood. It is he who has accomplished everything, counseled everything." When, at last, an hour comes in which he finds himself master of events, it is not so surprising to see Marmont take the course which settled once and for all these old private grudges.

And yet this argument does not explain quite everything about his sudden decision to take his regiments out of the fight. In spite of his resentments—resentments toward Napoleon that are noticeable also in many of the other marshals —Marmont had on the whole functioned well, or perhaps one should say he had always functioned well so long as he was serving under Napoleon's direct command. The whole development of his career shows, as Napoleon himself noted, that Marmont was the sort of man who felt himself strong, unbeatable, so long as he had behind him someone stronger still to bear the final responsibilities. Then the day comes when he sees his master toppling and suddenly must make the vital decision himself, with no one to back him. And at just this moment he is approached by another mind stronger than his own, in this case Talleyrand's, whereupon he reaches for the outstretched hand with the eagerness of a drowning man. Without an instant's delay he falls in with everything Talleyrand proposes.

What doomed him was the fact that his action bore consequences he could not foresee. Before he could think twice, the forces he had set in motion were spreading like the ripples on a pond, reaching points, touching persons he had failed to take into consideration. As we have seen, the virus of insubordination promptly seized on his generals. Their morale was low enough already, and once it was plain their commander had been negotiating with the allies and news of this might have reached Napoleon, they made the most of their chances to hurry the thing along.

That settled it for Marmont. The action his generals had taken could no longer be reversed. In part his undoing stemmed from his own flawed character, for the rest from

external forces he had released. As in so many other trage-
dies brought on by the victim's own doing, his downfall is
only in part the result of his yielding—as in the poem—to
the mermaid's tempting voice, and for the rest it is the result
of her active intervention. Goethe's fisherman is drowned by
a fatal combination of forces: *"Halb zog sie ihn, halb sank
er hin, und ward nicht mehr gesehen."* That is how it was
with Marmont.

But to come back to Caulaincourt, what of him? Was Fate
more kind to him than to Marmont?

Though his conduct may appear to have been the opposite
of Marmont's, the one too faithful to duty, the other hardly
dutiful enough, the effects were pretty much the same. Each
had been placed in a position of vital responsibility at a
critical moment, a turning point in history, and each had
proceeded to defeat his own and his monarch's real interests,
the one by failing to act, the other by acting. Both would live
to regret it. Both Caulaincourt and Marmont had failed to
do what cool deliberation should have dictated in men as
intelligent as they were. Caulaincourt could not bring himself to act when action would have saved what remained to
be saved, and Marmont took action of the most conclusive
sort when the logic of the situation demanded that he stand
fast.

By contrast Caulaincourt comes off relatively well, not
brilliantly, to be sure, but in nearly every respect better than
Marmont. One thing that had been working against him all
along was the damage his reputation had suffered as far back

as 1804. At that time he had quite innocently got himself involved in the unhappy affair of the Duc d'Enghien. Even though the involvement was peripheral—he had been one of the group which abducted Enghien from a royalist camp in neutral territory—he would always be regarded by some as at least in part responsible for the Duke's sad end. In Bourbon circles his guilt in this respect was accepted as truth beyond question, and not only was he considered an accessory to murder but a traitor to his class as well. The return of the Bourbons would naturally mean disaster for him.

Before that event occurred, however, Caulaincourt was to have an unexpected chance to regain the esteem he had lost at Chatillon, a chance he seized on with complete disregard for what the consequences to himself might be. What he had failed to do at Chatillon—the salvation of Napoleon by acting in defiance of Napoleon's express orders—he would accomplish now.

This was in Paris during the first days of April. The allied commissioners and Talleyrand were just sitting down to hammer out their settlement when, on April 8th, an urgent message from Napoleon, still at Fontainebleau, was handed to Caulaincourt. In it the Emperor said he regretted ever having signed the Act of Abdication. "The slow pace of the negotiations"—those were his words—could only mean he was about to be swindled, and in his opinion he would do better to make a fight of it even now, as many of his men were still completely devoted to him—the Guard and the troops in the cantonments around Lyon and in Italy. This being so, Caulaincourt must return to him at once the original of the

Act of Abdication which he, Caulaincourt, now had in his possession.

Caulaincourt never hesitated. He would under no circumstances surrender the document. He would protect the Emperor's true interests even if it cost him his life. Obviously the great man failed to realize that his personal safety now depended on the allies, that any act which resulted in further fighting would not only lead to civil war and dishonor him forever, but would bring about his destruction and very probably his death. Any attempt now to rescind the abdication would only be playing into the hands of the Provisional Government and give Talleyrand and his friends the excuse they were looking for to make an end of him. And so, fighting down that old, old impulse to obey an order given, and fully conscious of the danger he incurred by his disobedience, Caulaincourt replied that though he regretted it he could not in good conscience do a thing he considered so contrary to the Emperor's best interests, and at three in the afternoon on April 10th, in the Czar's salon in Talleyrand's house, he personally handed the Act of Abdication to the representatives of the allies and of the Provisional Government. Though this settled Napoleon's fate as Emperor, at least his life and security were made sure.

The Bourbons could hardly be pleased by this last service Caulaincourt had rendered Napoleon. On their return he was ordered to confine himself to his château and consider himself in exile, and there he remained for what turned out to be the rest of his life, devoting himself for the most part to writing his memoirs.

In 1821, a rather strange thing happened. Almost on the day Napoleon died, Caulaincourt observed in himself symptoms resembling those of the disease which carried off the Emperor, and in 1827, without having once taken any further part in public life, he died, stoically paying the price for having been in every situation of life exactly what he was.

4. OUDINOT

SNAP DECISIONS, SUCH AS THOSE ALREADY POINTED OUT in the careers of Caulaincourt and Marmont, are almost without exception faulty. Why this should be is not immediately clear, but it is an intriguing and undeniable fact. It would seem that when circumstances faced have never been faced before, when time presses and parallels in history or in the lives of others do not come easily to mind, decisions taken, as judged by their outcomes, prove generally to have been bad. It appears that the individual forced on short notice to decide what action to take, what course to follow, finds himself at a loss. Even if time is in no way a problem, even if he has had chances unlimited to consult with friends and colleagues, even after he has formulated a clear course of action in his own mind, he is still apt, when the moment for action comes, to forget all his plans, all his advices, all the recommendations, and let himself be carried away by instinct.

Instinct? Or if not instinct what is it that inspires the absurdities of behavior one sees so often in situations which ordinarily call for extensive reflection, which so often turn out to be the most decisive decisions taken in a lifetime? Examples of the folly of such decisions come to mind in almost everyone's personal experience. Striking ones can be found in almost any reading of history, but no happening fulfills the conditions just described better than those created by the invasion of a country by an enemy, say the panic that struck the South of France in June 1940 and the strange behavior of the thousands embroiled in it.

Italy had finally declared war and at that precise moment every Frenchman living on the Riviera, only miles from the Italian border, had to decide for himself what he was going to do, stay or flee. Many, including most of the best minds, did not hesitate for long. They loaded their cars with children and household goods and fled to the west even though they knew quite well, having discussed the eventuality among themselves and with friends, that the risk of falling into the hands of the German armies along the Atlantic was more to be feared than any encounter with the Italians, assuming an Italian invasion ever actually came. In the event these people were almost automatically following that deep-seated instinct which in animals and humans alike commands the avoidance of danger by flight, and no amount of thought, however well taken, is ever quite able to control the impulse. Many of the French who, a week later, returned to their homes in bullet-riddled cars were still wondering what exactly had inspired them to undertake this senseless adventure.

In some cases it is the ingrained response to habit that explains an absurdity of behavior. Admiral Byng, commander of the English Mediterranean squadron during the first days of the Seven Years War, had been condemned by court-martial for his failure to relieve Minorca and sentenced to be shot. Yet on the morning of his execution he took his usual antiscorbutic with only three hours of life remaining to him.

In contrast with cases such as these, cases in which blind instinct dictated behavior, the deliberate failure to act can have equally tragic consequences. Too many people threatened by Hitler's outrages consciously wasted whatever chance they had of escape. Talk of persecution, of deportation was being heard everywhere, and here again each had to decide whether he would go or stay, yet thousands threw away their lives by electing to stay, with the flimsy argument that "the danger was exaggerated in their particular cases, that things must certainly come right." These people could hardly plead ignorance. They knew all about concentration camps and gas chambers, about people being taken away in the night; they were on notice; and yet instead of fleeing they did what cornered animals so often do, they "played dead," they tried to make themselves invisible by keeping to their houses, their lairs as it were, never recognizing the real cause for their being unable to act logically.

But it doesn't take war or persecution to illustrate irra-

[67]

tional ways of acting under stress. Everyone has stories to tell about people caught in a shipwreck or a fire. With only seconds in which to decide what to abandon and what to save, the victim departs with a toothbrush, a pair of slippers, or a baby's rattle, leaving his important belongings behind him in full-packed drawers.

This inability to think objectively in moments of crisis tells much concerning the behavior of many men of fame whose dramatic and often foolish decisions at some vital turning point still baffle those who read their stories.

God knows, the situation that faced the men who were governing France on March 1st, 1815, was as bad as any shipwreck could be. Napoleon had escaped from Elba and was again on French soil. A chill ran through the ministries. Was it about to start all over again? Every Frenchman was involved, each had to make up his mind. Should he acclaim the returning Emperor or remain loyal to the Bourbon King, a question which for any man in high position was one of the first order. For him it was far more than a matter of sentiment, of approval or disapproval; he had to act, he must decide what part he was about to play, and this on the shortest notice.

The greater number of these men had served Napoleon, and under him acquired rank and wealth. After his fall they had tried to safeguard their positions, keep what they had by making their peace with Louis XVIII, but now? What were they to do? Observe their new oaths of office, or join the man who so often in the past had proved himself the master? On this could depend the difference between wealth and poverty, honor and disgrace. For many it could even be a matter of

Marechal Oudinto, Duc de Reggio
Litho Delpech
Collection Viollet

[69]

life or death, and it certainly would decide what the future was to be for them and for their families. Duty demanded loyalty to the King, but to turn one's back on the Emperor, already advancing on Paris—that could be disastrous.

At Metz, on the eastern frontier, Nicholas Charles Oudinot, marshal of France, one of the great figures of the Napoleonic wars, found himself facing this dilemma. During the twenty years he had served Napoleon he had never failed once in loyalty or devotion, never lacked in gratitude for favors granted him. Oudinot was a sober man. His title, Duke of Reggio, had never gone to his head; he loved war; he was a fighter all the way, wounded thirty-four times, so seriously the last time that he would carry the bullet to his grave. Ever the man of action, he had married again this last summer hardly a month after losing his wife of twenty years.

Oudinot was as much the realist in practical things as he had always been on the battlefield. Back in those dark days of March 1814 when he had brought his exhausted troops to Fontainebleau, he had been the first of the marshals to accept the hopelessness of the situation and demand an end to the fighting. A little later he had shown this practical side again by being among the first to declare for the Bourbons, among the first to offer his services to the new regime. Almost automatically he was rewarded by confirmation of his honors and titles and as a special distinction with the command of the elite regiments remaining from the "Old Guard," all men strongly attached to Napoleon personally and all longing for the days of their recent glory. They were known now as the "Royal Grenadiers and Chasseurs," and when Oudinot arrived at Metz where they were stationed he had been welcomed with the cheering reserved for old friends and comrades in arms.

With the news of Napoleon's landing and advance toward Paris, Oudinot found himself in a nasty position. His troops were jubilant; they were expecting, as was everyone else in Metz, that the general would assemble his men and march at the first opportunity to join the Emperor. As for himself, he couldn't help sharing his men's feeling; he disliked the new regime and, very much like his fellow veterans, was critical of nearly everything connected with it; he was attached to Napoleon by a hundred ties, but—he had taken service with the King. Could he ignore that?

The problem compounded itself when dispatches from Paris ordered him to march, intercept Napoleon and arrest him. It gave him a very bad moment, but there was no hesitation. Orders were orders and what may have made things easier was the letter received that same day from Ney, his brother marshal. It was a short, hastily written note, prudently worded but clear enough in its intentions. It ended with the words " . . . we must hold together against this common enemy of ours . . ." by whom he obviously meant Napoleon. Oudinot agreed. Having already fought down his natural inclinations, he was prepared to act as directed.

He could see, though, that he must tread softly. That night he assembled his officers and asked what they were going to do next morning when he faced the troops and called on them to join him in "Long live the King!"

After a long silence, one angry general spoke out.

"Try it, sir. Just try it."

Next morning he did just that. Standing before the

paraded guardsmen, he flourished his hat and shouted "Long live the King!" Silence greeted him. Then a young lieutenant stepped forward. "We will all answer, sir, to *Vive l'Empereur!*"

Oudinot's only rejoinder was an order to march, but before the day was over it was plain his men were only waiting the chance to go over to Napoleon. This left Oudinot little choice. That night he informed Paris he was handing over his command and would join his family at their Jean d'heure estate in Alsace.

Napoleon, once he was back in the Tuileries, responded to this "defection" by dismissing his old friend from the service, terminating his salaries and benefits, and restricting him for life to the Alsace estate, in other words disaster complete for Oudinot.

His family was stunned. So were his friends. What could have induced the old hero to act in such a way. There he had been, leader of this famous body of troops, men just waiting to throw themselves into the arms of their still idolized commander. How could he have remained deaf to the call of the man who made him, the man who now needed him so badly? One can still ask today, was it in fact the sense of loyalty, the sense of honor Oudinot always claimed it to have been, or was it with him as with Admiral Byng, as with the people who fled the Riviera, as with the victims of Hitler's persecution, an act dictated by a drive deeper than reason, an act of instinct, in his case the soldier's instinct to obey an order given?

Through the whole history of Oudinot's years of campaigning devotion to duty, conformance to orders, the soldier's obligation to obey so long as he wears the uniform, runs like a leitmotif. It is plain he was neither a man of imagination nor one given to breaking his head over a problem of ethics. When suddenly faced with the situation in Metz he did exactly what he had always done, what it was quite impossible for him not to do—his duty, in other words, to let himself be driven by that blind force within, which had prompted his every act these last years of his career, and so, with people everywhere waiting to see him take his old "grognards" into the imperial camp and lead them to another victory, he instead went quietly home and into retreat.

Luckily for him the days of Napoleon's restoration were to be few and by a turn of events he could hardly have foreseen, Oudinot would find himself once again in his former position of favor. Like Marmont he would be one of the Napoleonic commanders in good grace with the Bourbons, and would live out his remaining years in a manner he would insist was no more than due him for having served his king, for having done what duty called on him to do, an attitude which would have impressed him once as that of a used-up, tired old man.

5. NEY

However that may be, one may still ask if Oudinot's conduct at this time was quite as unnatural as that of Ney, his friend and fellow marshal. As his letter to Oudinot shows, Ney's first reaction to Napoleon's return was negative; he too protested his loyalty to the King and behaved in a fashion different from anything one would have expected from a fire-eater such as he. Very shortly, though, all that would change. While Oudinot stuck to his guns, Ney would reverse his attitude and take the course which led directly to his disgrace and tragic end.

The difference in the mental makeup of these two had been evident enough already, even as early as the first days following Napoleon's departure for Elba. Both had declared for

Louis XVIII and each had offered his services. Ney, too, had been confirmed in his honors and given carte blanche to have for himself any position he might fancy, but while Oudinot kept to his trade and settled down as a commander of troops in a garrison town, Ney seemed oblivious to his military past and devoted himself almost exclusively to being well received in the exalted circles of the Faubourg St. Germain. It was surprising, and at times a little painful, to see as fine a soldier as he going to such trouble to establish himself in the King's favor; it was shocking too to see how stricken the man could be when he did not quite succeed in this or when someone would repeat to him the words of the Duchess d'Angoulème, Marie Antoinette's only surviving child, when she wondered aloud "what Ney's wife, that niece of Madame Campan, a baker's daughter" was doing at court. To Ney there was nothing inconsistent in taking offense at the slurs of such people, and in his own habit of proclaiming himself everywhere as the confirmed democrat, a man of the people. Even while he was fawning on these courtiers he went right on castigating the snobberies of a nobility which "had won its titles by doing nothing more than to be born."

Where Oudinot was practical, Ney was romantic. By nature he was impetuous, impulsive and, as Napoleon himself remarked, unstable, characteristics which seemed to go hand in hand with those that had made his fame, that is, intrepidity, the ability to lead and inspire, the example he set at the head of the attacking column, his desperate stands when all seemed lost. No wonder he was known as "the bravest of the brave." There was however another side to the man. At times he could be suddenly discouraged and advise retreat

Marechal Ney in uniform
Collection Viollet

[77]

when to a Napoleon all odds seemed favorable, and in 1814 he characterized Napoleon in terms so bitter they sound strange on the lips of one so completely the child of the empire, one who for years on end had been the *enfant gâté* of Napoleon's headquarters.

Now word of Napoleon's return sent him into indignant apostrophes. He wrote all his old colleagues, harangued them repeatedly, and in general expressed himself more violently than even the King did. That man! Hadn't he agreed to step down, to take himself off the scene? What was he letting the country in for? A Napoleon on the throne! It could only mean disaster!

When the order came to report for active service, he asked for an audience with Louis, and without being solicited offered himself as the one best qualified to bring "the usurper" back to justice; when his offer was accepted and he was put in command of troops assigned to do just this, he boasted he would bring Napoleon back in an iron cage.

Forced marches soon brought his troops to the area where he could expect to encounter the "ogre," the region north of Lyon, and in the event it turned out that Lons-le-Saunier, a little mountain town halfway between there and Dijon, was the meeting place.

Here things took an unexpected turn. Ney found himself approached by the emissaries of Napoleon. He was handed a proclamation couched in Napoleon's old soul-stirring language which promptly moved him to tears. Meanwhile the troops had been talking with the people in the streets and, infected by their mood, were getting harder and harder to keep in hand. By next morning Ney decided he had no right to withhold the proclamation, and at precisely the moment he had finished reading it to the men Napoleon himself came walking up to the bivouac, alone, and addressed them all as old friends. Cheers broke out, and the marshal, already shaken, muttering something about not being able to hold back the sea with his hands, gave in. Without further effort to contain himself he joined in the "Vive l'Empereur!"

At the same moment all his pent-up resentments against the Bourbons seemed to burst forth. It was one long series of invectives against "this King who does nothing but get fatter and fatter," "this would-be commander in petticoats" who would never learn to handle soldiers, for whom soldiers were simply marionettes. Turning his back on those of his officers who refused to go along, he and his men joined the triumphal march back to Paris where news of the King's flight sent them into gales of laughter.

Waterloo changed all that. Charged with treason, Ney went into hiding, only to be arrested through his own carelessness. At his trial his counsel relied heavily on points like these, that the marshal could never have accomplished anything with troops so unwilling to support him, that sooner or later the Emperor would have had the upper hand in any case in a country so thoroughly won over to him, but few in the courtroom felt that these arguments, or any that followed similar lines of reasoning, had had much to do with influencing Ney to act as he had, and even Ney himself seemed to admit as much by his proud but almost despairing attitude as he faced his accusers. When General Bourmont, one of the officers who had refused to go over at Lons-le-Saunier, testified that the only way in which he could have

Marechal Ney after his execution
After Gérôme

prevented Ney from joining Napoleon would have been to shoot him, Ney's only rejoinder was, "I wish you had."

It is certainly idle to try to explain in terms of reasoned argument Ney's conduct at Lons-le-Saunier. The forces driving him can only be sought in the nature of the man himself, in his instincts and his inability to master them. He may have been the eagle on the battlefield, but he had always been regarded "a sitting duck" in the drawing room, the all-too-easy prey for any well-formulated point of view. Some of the events of those March days of 1814 as related earlier show the impressionability of the man, that day for instance when he, Caulaincourt and Macdonald faced the Czar hoping to reopen peace negotiations. From the first Ney had fallen in with the Czar's uncomplimentary observations on Napoleon. He seemed to forget that he and the others were there to gain what sympathy they could for the Emperor's cause, and it distressed his companions no end to hear him use words like "blind," "criminal," "tricky." A few days later, when the abdication had became a fact, he had delayed scarcely a minute in joining Talleyrand, not even bothering to return to Fontainebleau for the last farewell of his defeated chief.

Ney was an impulsive man, God knows, but for all that he had been one of the most brilliant, most reliable field officers of the Empire, and when placed in command of the expedition sent to intercept Napoleon he can't have failed to understand its all-out importance. His decision at Lons-le-Saunier makes no sense at all, unless one takes into account his background and personality, that and the agonizing circumstances under which this decision was made—time lacking and action called for immediately. It was the sort of situation in which even the most superior individual some-times behaves as if for a moment his inhibitions had lapsed, his brain ceased to operate, with only instinct, the primal side of the man left functioning. Perhaps Ney may have seen it that way himself as they led him out to face the firing squad.

6. LOUIS, KING OF FRANCE

THE MENTAL SHOCK THAT CAME WITH NAPOLEON'S RE-
turn from Elba was not restricted to the circle of his former
associates, his one-time officials and marshals. Probably no
one in all France was more affected by it than the King
himself, Louis XVIII, and for no one was the dilemma more
harassing.

When first told of Napoleon's landing, Louis merely
shrugged. What chance did Monsieur Bonaparte imagine he
had? You had only to read the papers; France was so united
against him he would soon be glad to be back in little Elba
again. Besides, Ney was about to take care of everything. But
as the days passed and the Emperor moved farther and
farther north, on that day especially when news of Ney's

defection finally reached Paris, Louis began to realize he must act. He must decide what his course was going to be, whether he would stay and fight, whether he would leave; and if the choice was to fight, at what place should the stand be made, and if to leave, leave for what destination and when.

After hours spent with staff and advisers he came to the conclusion it would be better to stand fast, but where? No one seemed to agree on that. Some held for the Pyrenees, some said it should be the West, others the North, but then on March 18th Napoleon reached Fontainebleau, and Louis realized he had no more time to waste. Shaking off his advisers, he took the hero's resolve—he would stand where he was, defend the Tuileries against all comers, and if Fate willed it, "die like a soldier."

Orders went out to every batallion in the region to assemble at the palace; artillery was to be mounted, the gates and terrace fortified. Marmont, Macdonald, Berthier—all three had remained loyal—would be in charge, but before going into action they must attend a meeting in the King's salon. The atmosphere was solemn. Together with the Prince d'Orleans, Artois, and the Duke de Berry they stood before Louis, shoulder to shoulder, and swore fidelity to the throne, fidelity unto death. The King in turn addressed his loyal followers in no less glowing words. "Let us unite under this our sacred banner; the heir of Henry IV will lead you, and behind us will march every right-thinking man in France," to which the courtiers responded in unison, "On our honor we swear to live and die faithful to our King and to his charter which insures the happiness of all."

It was all most impressive; tears flowed, arms rose in salute, but as the day drew to a close, what in fact did happen? Around six, Louis stepped into the first of several carriages, all heavily loaded with *pretiosae,* and headed for his first stop, Lille, with Ghent to follow. In the carriage with him was a trunkful of gold, and guarding it and him were those same men who had vowed to die fighting at his side. To make certain doubly certain, they had provided themselves with an escort of three hundred dragoons whom Berthier had managed to scrape together at the last minute.

What lay behind his Majesty's sudden volte-face? Did it reflect a reasoned estimate of his chances of success or of his readiness to die? Not at all. One look at his past, his real nature, tells it all.

In his younger days Louis had been, in appearance at least, quite another man than the one he was now. As Count de Provence, Louis XVI's oldest brother, "Monsieur" as he was called, he was perhaps the most spoiled and envied man in the realm. So long as his sister-in-law, Marie Antoinette, remained childless, he was heir presumptive to the French throne. He enjoyed this enviable position most thoroughly, but alas, it all ended that day in 1778 when the Queen, after seven years of marriage, bore her husband their first child. Provence's disappointment went deep, so deep that even his best efforts could not conceal it. In a letter dated October 5, 1778, to Gustav III, King of Sweden, he made no secret of how it affected him.

"You may have heard of the recent change involving my future," it began. "I have been able to keep my feelings to myself, though. A show of joy would have been taken for insincerity, as it rightly would have been, because in all honesty, and you may believe me in this, I could feel none . . ."

Even so, his hopes refused to die and over the succeeding years very slowly, a bit here, a bit there, he busied himself seeking to make intrigue accomplish what nature had failed to do. Through this whole period that preceded the Revolution he was undoubtedly one of the agents most responsible for the growing hostility toward King and Queen, toward Marie Antoinette especially, and his scheming was so persistent it may well have been one of the factors hastening the end of the regime. When the Revolution finally did begin he kept himself very much in the background, quietly watching events, always hoping—as did his cousin the Prince d'Orleans, for quite different reasons—that public sentiment would turn his way. Then the King attempted his abortive flight to Varennes, and recognizing that the royalist cause had been badly compromised, Provence fled too, not with the King, but quite on his own and in quite a different direction. Establishing himself at Coblentz on the Rhine, he made that place a center for royalist agitation, contributing thereby in no small measure to his brother's imprisonment and death.

With the King gone, and the Dauphin missing and apparently dead too, Provence took himself to be the legitimate King of France, a title he continued to use during the whole of the Napoleonic era. Over that same time he continued his activities, his strategy consisting in the main of attempts to bribe the men heading the French government: Barras during the Directory, Napoleon himself in the period that fol-

Louis XVIII (Comte de Provence) before he became king, in 1791, during his flight out of France
Collection Viollet

[87]

Louis XVIII as king
Collection Viollet

[88]

lowed. Both were offered magnificent positions and enormous incomes if only they would step down and accept second place.

For twenty long years the never-despairing head of the house of Bourbon filled his time with this futile sort of activity. Grown fat and gouty, he never attempted, not even once, any part that might be called heroic or even faintly energetic, though from time to time chances to do so did come his way. Rather than that he patiently bided his time and in the end found himself rewarded. Only days after Napoleon's fall he entered Paris with the allied armies and promptly showed his remoteness from reality by making his appearance in the uniform of an eighteenth-century general with gold epaulets so enormous that the Parisians gaped and then started to laugh when they saw his train togged out similarly in antiquated splendor. This might have taught Louis something. Obviously it did not. He continued to behave as if the quarter of a century just past had never been, and he made himself hated by tactless favoritism and his efforts to restore a state of things which clearly had ceased to be. Is it surprising then that with Napoleon back from Elba, and faced with a decision to fight or flee, he should have found it impossible to be the strong man he would have liked to be; for him was it not the natural thing to find again a quiet place of exile and do there what the Bourbons had always done best—wait and see?

Once he was reestablished on the throne after Waterloo, Louis must have regretted this headlong flight in the dark. His advisers may well have felt a little foolish too; too late they discovered how little they could expect from the man, one who at each turning in his life had done exactly this same thing, sought out the safest hiding place in which to wait for the day when the French throne would in fact be his.

Often Louis, flattered and pampered in the magnificent salons of his palace, may have felt that in making his impulsive decision of March 19th he had lost, once and for all, any possibility of gaining that popularity he so much craved, a popularity he never ceased to hope would blot out the memory of Napoleon. Instead it had brought him the scorn of the entire French people, a scorn which would attach to him even beyond the grave.

7. THE DUEL

NO LESS SENSELESS THAN THOSE ACTS OF COWARDICE OR near-cowardice which compromise or destroy the success of a life, are those acts of excessive bravery which defy reason in the same way, acts committed without time taken to weigh the chances of success or to consider the risks of failure, acts which for all their nobility may appear to others as little different from insanity.

Often these acts are, however, an expression of the highest human emotions—the mother entering a burning house to rescue her child, the man plunging into a river to save his favorite dog or go under with it. Acts like these, in spite of their impulsive nature, may not be, strictly speaking, illogical or even unreasonable, but there are still other varieties of brave acts, less common and less natural, perhaps, that seem only to spring from mysterious forms of mental aberration. In these bravery seems pointless. They appear to be inspired by no rational aim, and if anything is accomplished, if some end is effected, it is utterly disproportionate to the effort made, the risks involved.

One recalls the mad bravery of certain Polish dragoons who at almost certain risk of drowning leaped their horses into the Vistula to impress a frozen-faced Napoleon who had just made his appearance on the farther bank. Probably fierce momentary enthusiasm, the infection of mass emotion, are the driving forces in cases such as this—as indeed they were with Ney—but it can also be that quite other drives, deeply embedded, suddenly take over and destroy what has been until then a well-ordered way of life.

Frederick, Count of Darmstadt, tells in his memoirs an incident that happened during the retreat from Russia in 1812. Feeling himself at the end of his strength, he begged the four Hessians of his escort to find some way to shield him from the terrible wind which made all rest impossible. Without hesitation the men removed their coats and fastened them on poles, making a makeshift tent for their exhausted commander. In the morning when he awoke, his call brought no answer. Looking outside, he saw his men lying there, all four of them frozen to death.

In instances like these a feeling of duty, an urge to sacrifice oneself, perhaps simply a moment of great exaltation, blots out all the considerations which normally determine what a man will or will not do. Impulses surging up from the deepest recesses of the being override the instinct of self-preservation and sweep away all thought of the future. Looking back on it, supposing hindsight were granted to them, the participants would never believe themselves capable of such selflessness; they would almost certainly feel their sacrifice had gone beyond anything the situation really called for.

What baffles one even more, however, is to see acts of reckless bravery—and in certain cases acts of cowardice—occurring in the lives of otherwise cool-headed, straight-thinking individuals faced with an event they imagine they have well prepared themselves to deal with. At this point self-control eludes them and they do the very thing they have sworn they will never, never do. For weeks a village school-teacher had been giving instruction to his neighbors on the laws of warfare—this was in the north of France in the spring of 1940—especially on the rules governing conduct of civilians caught in a battle zone, on their duty to refrain from taking part in any fighting they might happen to witness. For this, he stressed, the penalty was death. A day came, however, when the worst happened, when his village was overrun by the enemy and he saw people being killed and houses going up in flames. Instantly all theory was forgotten. As if possessed, he snatched up a rifle from a dying soldier and took his place in the fighting line until retreat sounded, the troops fell back, and the village was abandoned to the enemy. Taken gun in hand, the teacher was put against the wall and shot in full view of his fellow villagers whom he had been at such pains to instruct.

The case of Humbert de la Tour du Pin illustrates the point even better. The courage shown by this young man seems totally uncalled for, senseless really, horrifying in its tragic uselessness, and yet considering his background, who he was, perfectly understandable.

By now it is 1816. Napoleon has gone, this time forever. The wars are over and Europe returned to normalcy. Humbert's father, the Marquis de la Tour du Pin, had in recent years been a member of the imperial *corps diplomatique* while his twenty-five-year old son had been eating his heart out as subprefect in an insignificant provincial town of northern France. Napoleon's fall released him from this drudgery and very shortly he was given the long-desired military assignment, in this instance aide-de-camp to Marshall Victor, Duke of Belluno, one of the heroes of the just-finished wars.

The position in the messroom of a newcomer such as he was hardly likely to be easy at a time when most of the members were hardened veterans, men risen from the ranks who had earned their epaulets at Austerlitz, Friedland, Wagram.

On this particular day as Humbert came into the guardroom, he ran into one of Victor's other aides, a certain Major Malandin, an older officer, well over forty and the survivor of fifteen years of combat. Malandin was perhaps a bit on the rough side, a not-too-well educated man, intensely proud of his rank and decorations, but not a bad sort at heart. In an awkward attempt at joviality he greeted his new associate with a rather silly and tactless remark about the frogs on his uniform not being in quite the right place. Affronted, enraged, Humbert was about to give him as good as he got, but just here the marshal himself walked in and sent Malandin off on some errand. As a result, the quarrel, if one can call it that, was not settled on the spot as it normally would have been, and for Humbert this couldn't be the end.

That night, at home, he reported the incident to his father, presenting it, however, in a hypothetical form, as if a young friend were involved. His question: What should the offended party do?

The Marquis, never suspecting his son was talking of himself, didn't hesitate. "Your friend must challenge the fellow."

"And if the man offers an apology?"

"He must not accept it. Don't forget—he has never been in battle. He must show he's as good a soldier as any of them, afraid of nothing."

That same evening Humbert challenged Malandin. The others in the mess were stunned. All wanted to mediate the thing, and even Malandin himself, somewhat embarrassed, came forward to say very gallantly that he had been in the wrong, that he was sorry. None of this had the least effect on Humbert. They must fight, he insisted; and having the offended party's right of the choice of weapons, he announced they would fight with pistols. The others, knowing Malandin's skill with the pistol, tried to dissuade him. If he must fight, choose sabers, but Humbert would have none of it, and all efforts to put a stop to the affair having ended in failure, nothing remained but to proceed.

Early next morning, in the Bois de Boulogne, the two took their places, but at the very last moment as they stood there twenty-five paces apart, ready to fire, Malandin signaled that he would like to speak. White of face and in a voice that trembled he began:

"Monsieur de la Tour du Pin, in the presence of these

gentlemen I repeat I am sorry for having spoken as I did. Two brave men should never have to kill each other for so slight a thing."

There was a sigh of relief. All present assumed that this ended the affair, and looked on with satisfaction as Humbert, after a second's hesitation, walked across to where Malandin was waiting. Then, instead of offering his hand as everyone was expecting, he raised an arm and struck Malandin across the face with the butt of his pistol.

"You will hardly refuse to fight now," he said, and with that went back to his place.

Malandin's face was distorted, as much by stupefaction, he recalled later, as by anger.

"He's a dead man," they heard him say. At the signal to fire, Malandin crossed his arms and awaited Humbert's shot, which missed; then raising his arm, he muttered, "Poor child, poor mother," and shot him through the heart.

How account for such stubbornness when satisfaction, the only thing to be gained in a duel, has already been offered?

In some part it was almost certainly the child in the man, the child who finds himself ringed with onlookers and imagines he must prove himself. But for the rest it can only spring from his personal history, from his deep-seated longings, the yearning of a man brought up on tales of heroism during long years of military effervescence and by circumstance excluded from the world of the uniform, the yearning of one who has realized early in life that he is to have no part in the grandeur of the age, yet still hopes to make himself "one of them." Now at last he is an officer; now at last, even if the wars are over, opportunity knocks. When Malandin offers him his apology he feels cheated and resolves not to let this chance slip away. Without regard for all that is at stake, for himself and his opponent, he strikes the latter in the face, the ultimate provocation, and as he goes back to his place ready to fire, for one split second he sees himself a member of the Guard formed up in square to receive the charging cavalry.

Here again, as it was with Caulaincourt and Marmont, with Ney, Oudinot and Louis, the decisive impulse comes rising up out of nowhere, out of the distant past, the offspring of some long-forgotten trauma, some emotion half-dreamt and never quite experienced, which has come to be a part of the soul's makeup, hopes, fears, longings which demand to be followed blindly while the warnings of reason and objective consideration are wantonly thrust aside.

Decisions of this kind, violent, unreasoned, contrived on the spur of the moment, taken in the face of the clearest realization of what is at stake both for now and for the rest of life, are undoubtedly seen as frequently in ordinary day-to-day living as in the lives of heroic or historical figures. A girl turns her back on the man she loves because of some fancied slight and marries instead one with whom she knows she can never be happy. A man abandons a cherished career because an unexpected proposal seems suddenly to offer something far more tempting, and in so doing ruins all chance of giving his life the meaning he had always expected it to have.

Life, when studied closely, is rarely logical in its unfoldment; it seldom permits the completion of a well-ordered plan, seldom fulfills what its beginnings seemed to promise.

Too often, at some sudden forking of the road, it misses its true course and loses itself in a morass of unrelated problems —all of which confirms what André Gide, that pessimistic knower of man, concluded after examining his own and his friends' careers under the magnifying glass: "The most decisive acts of our lives, the ones most apt to decide the whole of our future, are almost always unreasoned," and, one might add, the result of what to other eyes seem to have been futilities.

THE FURIES

THE FURIES

THE FIRST FANFARE IN THE STREET, THE FIRST CLATTER
of hoofs on the cobbles, brought Mariette running to the
window.

"The horseguards! The yellow riders!" She was jubilant.

It was a squadron of Kellerman's dragoons, brilliant in the
new uniforms given them for the part they had played that
summer at Marengo, the victory Bonaparte wished above all
else to dramatize. He seemed determined to make the Parisians conscious of all it signified, how for the second time in
three years North Italy had been won for the land of the New
Ideas and a much-desired peace secured as well. The famous
17th Division, its dragoons, chasseurs and cuirassiers, had
been brought back to Paris and quartered in the town to keep

national spirits high and at the same time insure order. The people loved their heroes. From the shouts and cheering that greeted them now you might have thought their commander in chief was riding ahead.

Topino-Lebrun hadn't left his easel. When Mariette sent a glance his way and repeated, softly this time, "The yellow riders," he barely moved as he stood there studying his canvas. That he despised these stagy demonstrations she knew, but to ignore them as he did, to show his feelings so openly, that was a mistake. It was unreasonable, dangerous even, at a time like this with the whole town running half-mad with enthusiasm for its new idol.

"If just to please me, Topino. Come here. Let people see you, cheer a little, wave! Please! With all these rumors going around you ought to."

His reply was merely another brush stroke, and unhappily she turned back to the scene in the street.

Mariette was one of those Parisian girls who seem to be endowed from birth with a wealth of common sense, an instinct for doing whatever the occasion demands, girls with a minimum of schooling perhaps, girls from the most modest of environments—hers was the janitor's loge—who still surprise with the uncanny depth of their understanding, and for all their lack of real beauty possess charm almost in excess.

Mariette knew her world and never hesitated to use that knowledge to be as gay as any of the rest, but she could be serious too and deeply devoted where the heart was involved. She loved her painter. For all his eccentricities he was her god, and while marriage might be no more than a far-off dream, she felt that everything that concerned him concerned her as well. He was so imprudent! No one could be so reckless in the things he said and did! Why did he have to be so outspoken when everyone else was keeping his mouth shut and his opinions inside his head? And yet she couldn't help it, she loved him for this very thing, the complete sincerity, those candid blue eyes which looked at you so thoughtfully, with a thoughtfulness that more and more seemed to be second nature to him.

Sometimes she wondered. A man so young, barely thirty, why should he be so abstracted, so serious? Topino-Lebrun was a coming name in the world of art, his future could hardly be brighter; his paintings were beginning to sell and his latest had been accepted by the Salon, an unheard-of thing for a man not in good standing with the government. Why was it, then? Why was it that in spite of success he seemed to be even more withdrawn, especially these last weeks? It worried her and at times she would ask herself if it might not be that his state had something to do with that story a few days back when he had asked her, in almost stifled tones, to pick up a package for him at that little shop on the corner, that odd little shop where the blinds were always drawn, if this package might not, in some obscure way, have something to do with his all too well-known political leanings. Her heart had been heavy ever since, and now, this morning, his lack of response, the fierce expression in the eyes, the scorn you could feel beneath his silence . . . it somehow filled her with apprehension.

The dragoons moved on, the street was quiet, but she couldn't make herself leave the room. Closing the window and picking up a cloth, she turned to the row of canvases

[103]

leaning against the wall and began to dust them, trying to cover up the silence meanwhile with a stream of chatter about what they were saying in the street.

"You can't believe half of it, I suppose. Lots of it's nonsense probably, but I think it's better to know what's going on."

He still said nothing but did seem to be listening, so she went on. Yes, the story of what had happened last night was coming out at last and that was perhaps why you saw so many soldiers. Both Arena and Ceracchi were in jail. They had been caught right there in the Opera after the attempt on Bonaparte and—she sent a rapid glance Topino's way—a number of other conspirators had been rounded up too. And there was something else he should know. It hadn't all come through her mother this time; she had heard it herself. Last night. That had been practically all they could talk about. Yes, at Duval's. And the excitement was something hard to imagine. They were all going on about what a scandal it was, trying to kill *him,* the one man the country couldn't spare, the first consul, their great general. Imagine if they'd brought it off! That's how the talk had gone. Fright and consternation, and then threats and abuse no end.

This time Topino put down his brush.

"Duval's? You went there again?"

"But Topino—"

"Without asking me, telling me? I thought I'd made it clear—you were never to set foot in that house again."

"Oh, Topino . . . " She brought her hands together. "You don't like him, I know, but think how it was. Citoyen Duval needed me. He was giving this party and help isn't easy to come by anymore, not for parties in the big houses anyway, and mother was wondering, what with everything costing so much, why I shouldn't . . . and then she was saying, too, we really ought to try to be nice. Citoyen Duval had always been kind to his neighbors. Well, anyway—even you'd admit he is an important man, and you never can tell when he. . . .

. . . Just take his house. You should see it, all done over, just since that other time I was there. Silk, bronze, gold everywhere! And he *is* nice, you know, very nice, and very polite, that way he has with you, almost fatherly. And he pays well too. I got six francs, and they told us we could keep the costumes, nice dresses really! We were all in gray and pink, ever so smart, I tell you, six girls all in gray and pink."

"So that's how he rigged you out." Topino squeezed out half a tube of pink alongside the gray already on his palette and considered the effect with a grin. "I don't know what the Luynes colors were but I'll bet anything they were gray and pink. That's 'Monsieur' Duval for you. Be like the man whose house you've taken over, ape the style of Monsieur le Duc. Who knows, before long he may be a duke himself. Now please. Leave those canvases alone. I've told you a dozen times, you shouldn't be seen going in and out of here so much. Please now, Mariette. Get along with you. Go!"

"He's rich, you can't imagine how rich." She went on with the dusting as if he hadn't spoken. "He's the biggest man in the quartier. Knows everything about everything." She straightened up, turned, and lowering her voice, "You might as well know the truth, Topino. I didn't go because of mother. I did it because I thought I ought to. I thought it might be a good thing to have been there, to hear, to know . . . ”

Topino cut her off. “If the man you’ve promised to marry has asked you not to go there, seriously, repeatedly, why would—”

“Look, Topino.” She came a step closer. “This time was different. I couldn’t help thinking I had to . . . for your sake . . . for you, you! to hear what they might be saying, to know if they were talking about you, because there *has* been talk about you, you know. Passing cakes and wine to people, important people, comes in handy sometimes. You hear a lot that’s worth hearing and—and . . . ” She stopped.

“Well say it. Say it.”

“I might as well tell you. They did talk about you.”

He looked sharply at her. “You’re sure?”

“Yes, your paintings. Not in a very kind way, either. They didn’t like them, I mean the things you paint. And there was a lot of talk about a caricature that’s being shown around everywhere, something they think only you could have done. Then someone mentioned your living across the street, and there was talk about squaring things with you—that’s the word they used—even getting rid of you, no matter how; yes, that’s exactly what one of them said. Oh, Topino, it was so mean, so nasty. I can’t get it out of my head.”

“My work doesn’t please them?” He shrugged. “You can’t please everybody.”

“They kept coming back to one painting. The Death of . . . Gracchus? Is that the way you say it? They kept going on and on about it.”

[106]

"The city of Marseilles owns it."

"Well, these people don't like it. Why do you have to paint things like that, Topino? Things that rub people the wrong way? Why? You never want to tell me. Gracchus. Who was this Gracchus anyway?"

"Didn't they tell you about him at school? No? Well, Gracchus was a Roman, a very good Roman, one who hated tyranny."

"But, Topino, why not paint what people want, what people would like to have in their houses? You could make heaps of money. Ever so much. You could buy a house of your own! We could marry!"

"I thought I told you to get along with you. Yes, I did tell you. A girl shouldn't be seen hanging around a painter's atelier."

Coming very close, she let her voice drop.

"Topino, sometimes I don't understand. Sometimes you're like a stranger, I feel as if there were a wall between us. The things you paint. Death, blood. Why those? Why those things always? Explain it to me. Tell me. I'd feel so much better." And when there was no reply, "You mustn't treat me this way, like a child. It isn't fair. I know you don't care about money, you don't care if they buy your things or not, but why—why do you want to paint those things? Why do you *like* to paint them, because I can see you do like it!" And when he stood there, looking past her, "They're frightening," she said. "If I were a painter it wouldn't be like that. I'd be looking for sun and flowers. I'd paint what's beautiful, what I liked to see, what made me happy. Why not be like Greuze, or Gerard, or Ingres—paint girls, nice girls with beautiful bodies, or fine people with beautiful faces?"

Topino stood there, silently contemplating his brushes.

"Answer me, Topino! Don't you know why?"

He turned to her, nodding his head as if speaking to himself.

"I think one paints the things one loves too much."

"Too much? How can you ever love too much?"

"There *are* things that can be too beautiful. So beautiful they're almost past bearing. But what choice have we? We have to live with these things, the things that are almost too much, beautiful or terrible. That goes for the painter too. Painting's his way of trying to make peace with such things."

"But what about a Watteau? He was always painting girls, garden parties, love scenes. You don't mean he thought all that so terrible? And Ingres too. It's the same with him today."

Topino backed off a few steps, had a long look at his canvas, and finally, in a tone slow and pensive, let the words come, as if trying to clarify for himself something he had never been able to quite think through.

"Yes. Love scenes can be terrible. Yes. They can. For certain people anyway. Watteau kept busy half his life painting love scenes. You'd have said he was obsessed by them. But Watteau was a sick man and girls would have nothing to do with him, so he painted men trying to conquer these same girls, men at the point of raping them—which was probably Watteau's way of making it easier to bear what would otherwise have been unbearable. And Ingres? When he sketches a girl like that one he calls *La Source* he's really telling us that he's haunted by the wish to possess a girl

[108]

who's still a virgin. Or the same with *Le Vase Brisé* . . . "

Then, as if awakening and finding Mariette standing there, listening, "I told you you shouldn't be here," and as she still made no move to go, "All right then, if there's no other way." He picked up his hat. "I'll go down with you."

Having seen her as far as her mother's little ground-floor apartment he went on into the street and around the block to the nearest *marchand de couleur.* They were out of the shades he wanted, but seeing a stack of gazettes he asked if by any chance they had the *Moniteur.* The man handed him a copy with a grin.

"Color enough in the news today, citizen. Even for non-painters, wouldn't you say?"

"What is it you're talking about?"

"You don't know? Really? Well, well. Certain people are going to be keeping their hands on their necks all day just to be sure things there are still in one piece."

The smirk on the man's face was enough to send Topino out the door. He almost ran home and up the stairs to his room, where he plunged into his work, keeping at it steadily, feverishly, until a knock came and Mariette slipped in.

"I'm sorry," she whispered, "I had to—Oh my God, the way you look!" Paint spattered his apron, hands and trousers; his eyes were burning, shot with blood. "Two o'clock and you haven't even thought of eating. Oh, Topino. You sit here all day, never even budging and all the time . . . " She bit her lips.

"What?"

" . . . things are happening. People talking. Everybody's talking about that thing . . . "

[109]

"Don't speak in riddles."

" . . . that thing at the Opera, Topino. Last night. Police have been going around the street all day, yes, right down here, prowling, questioning. Do something, Topino. Please. Come down with me. Let people see you. Talk, say something, anything, that you're glad it ended the way it did, that you're as happy as they are, as relieved." And with a sidelong glance, "You *are* relieved, aren't you?"

"Relieved because we're saddled with Bonaparte for God knows how long?"

"But imagine! Suppose they'd killed him." And when he merely shrugged and went back to work again, "What is it you hate so about Bonaparte? Maybe he is harsh sometimes, but what else would you expect from a general who wants everything back in order again. I say it's a good thing we've got him. Everybody's laughing, gay! Paris is Paris! We can laugh, joke, feel good, feel proud. People are sure it's all going to get better and better! The mistake you make, Topino, is never wanting to see him. I told you about that day at the Carrousel, how he came in on his white horse with the Mameluk right behind and General Murat all covered with gold? The way he slid out of the saddle, the quick way he walked off into the palace. Topino, if you'd only take the trouble to see him just once . . . "

"Oh, stop it. Running after men on horseback, gaping at breastplates, plumes, cheering, shouting, as if guns were all we needed, as if guns were going to settle everything that's wrong in the world."

"They did settle a few things in Italy, didn't they?"

"Can't you get it through your head? Generals may be all

right on the battlefield, but in the Luxembourg, running the country, they're a disaster, a disaster for everybody, you, me, every soul who cares a rap about freedom." And suddenly putting down his brushes, "Can't you, and the rest of you, see he's bringing back all the plagues we thought we were rid of, the Duvals, the valets, the lace, the silk stockings? Arena was no fool. He saw the whole thing." And then, as if in pronouncing the name he had gone too far, he stopped and turned back to his canvas.

The name he had blurted out had had its effect. She stood there looking at him for a long, long moment. At last, haltingly, she said, "So—you believe—Arena was right?" And when he said nothing: "Right to do what he did?"

"Brutus got rid of Caesar for the sake of liberty. You don't blame Brutus, do you?"

Instead of an answer there was a long pause.

"Sometimes I can't help wondering, Topino," she finally said. "I love you. You know I do. I love you with all my heart, but . . . there's a side of you that escapes me. Your taking up with people, getting mixed up with people like—like—oh, yes, you've been seen with . . . "

A whistle sounded in the street. In an instant she was at the window, waving to someone below. Topino's head came up.

"What's that? What are you doing?"

She came back, slowly. "I know you're going to scold me." She stood there facing him. "But—Topino, I had to. Listen. You don't seem to realize it, but something had to be done. Yes. Now. Right now. I thought of Lemot. I've been thinking of him all these last days. Lemot's your friend. He likes you, you like him and you were close in the old days. I had to tell him."

"Tell him? What? In the devil's name, what?"

"What? Topino, my love. You ask that, what? Down there in the street they're talking about you. They have been for days; but now, since last night it's a different kind of talk. The police are all over the place, asking questions, eavesdropping, and last night at Duval's they were saying that with Arena in jail you'd be next, it would be easy—you hear? —easy to get rid of you. Yes, that's what they were saying."

Topino groaned. "Lemot. You went to him . . . "

"Don't be angry." She clasped her hands. "All morning all kinds of people have been wondering about you, so wasn't it a good idea to go to Lemot? He was here two weeks ago —I didn't tell you then—but he came looking for you. You were out—and afterwards he sat down, talked. He was worried, he said, and what he told me worried me too. He said you'd been mentioned in connection with certain people they had their eye on. I promised I'd let him know the minute anything . . . "

"And he's coming here? Now? Oh my God!"

"Topino, it's the best thing that could happen. The minute I felt things were—well, going wrong. . . . Oh, Topino, you still won't see it, but—"

"My God, Lemot here!" He was pacing the floor.

"But why take it that way? He's your friend. And he counts. He's on good terms with nearly everyone. A great artist! A famous man! Lemot and his sculpture—everybody knows them. He'll know what to do; he's the kind of man who can put the whole thing straight, the kind who . . . "

There was a knock. "Please, Topino. Please. Everything's going to be all right."

Before he could stop her she had opened the door and Lemot walked in. At the same time Mariette managed to slip past him and out.

"This time I've caught you!"

Arms outstretched, Lemot came over to Topino, embraced him and took both his hands in his. His smile was warm and so infectious Topino couldn't help smiling too. Lemot was no taller than he, but more stockily built and with a look of solidity which Topino definitely lacked. They were about the same age, but unlike Topino, Lemot obviously enjoyed life and had been doing well for himself. His clothes were finely tailored, the moustache neatly trimmed, he had his hair combed back in the latest fashion. Somehow he radiated success, success and good nature.

Taking Topino by the shoulders, he held him at arm's length. "That face, those eyes. Upset? Troubled? Cheer up! We'll get things fixed for you, we'll have it all straightened out in no time."

"You—here. It's madness, François. Get out as fast as you can," and pushing him toward the door, "Go! Please. For heaven's sake, go!"

"Easy, easy." Lemot pulled away and drew up a chair for himself. "Sit down, man. Sit down. There can't be *that* much hurry, not for the moment, anyway, and we do have things to talk about. Mind if I take off my coat? Warm in here."

"You mustn't stay. You can't afford to be seen in this place."

"And why not?" Lemot got up from his chair and with the

[113]

greatest care draped his coat over the back of the couch.

"But don't you know why? It's madness. Idiotic!"

"It's nice to be a little idiotic at times." Quietly, Lemot sat down and stretched his legs. "How long has it been, seven years? Yes, almost seven years exactly. Everybody was saying then you were an idiot to be putting in a word for a chap named Lemot when that silly fellow managed to get himself in trouble with the Jacobins. And what happened? You did get yourself a black mark with Robespierre, and God knows that was no laughing matter in those days. But you did it. Yes, you did it, and so—here am I, François Lemot, alive and well, spared by the guillotine, and that's why I'm here with you . . ." Topino had gone back to the easel and was mechanically painting again. "For God's sake, man, put down those brushes. Listen to me now and listen carefully. I'm here to save you."

"From what?"

"Are you serious?"

"I wasn't active in any of it."

"Look. There's no point in sticking your head in the sand. They've got Arena, they've got Ceracchi. They're looking for Demerville, and they know pretty well who the others are."

"I tell you, I had nothing to do with it."

"Fouché's men don't think so. For them it's not so much who was in it or who wasn't. You have to realize the kind of times we live in. They're after everything that smacks of liberalism, even faintly liberal. That's Bonaparte's line. Back to order. Today Jacobin, even Republican, is a bad word, and Arena's stupidity is made to order for them, gives them

[114]

their chance to make an example. Fouché's gloating over it."

"And what, pray tell, has all this got to do with me?"

"Think a little, Topino! If there was nothing else about you, what about all those years? Your past, your record?"

"I thought it was forgiven and forgotten."

"Forgotten? You and Robespierre, how close you were? You think all that's forgotten? And that later story, your tie-in with Babeuf? All right; you being a painter, they pardoned you, let you go. They let you leave the country, and then the Directory went under and they let you come back and settle down again, but even so, you think that wipes the slate clean? That they haven't got you on their list?"

"If it's so, it's bad, but what could I do?"

"You ask? Instead of sticking to work you get mixed up in this. It's preposterous! Unbelievable! Crazy! After being saved, not once but twice, you get involved again, this time in this half-witted affair. My God, what were you thinking of? I wish you'd tell me. After giving your word, promising you'd stick to painting and forget politics!"

Topino scraped away at his palette, saying nothing.

"You did give your word, Topino! We all thought you meant it!"

"I did mean it. Believe me, I did. I've tried very hard." He looked out the window as if he saw the years passing. "I did the best I could, but then . . ."

"Well, so be it. You did keep your word, for a while anyway—a year, two years. I guess you tended strictly to business, and so far as one could tell from my end of town you've done a lot of good work, very good work. It all seemed to be coming along fine, and how happy that made me; you don't know how happy. And then all at once—rumors, rumors . . ."

"My God, François, you aren't blind, you know what's happening. A dictator's running the country. Bonaparte's bringing back the whole dirty mess, the emigrés, the traitors, the system. Nobles in office again, swindlers getting rich. Duval there across the street calling himself a wool merchant . . . what is he? An army contractor, piling up money faster than Monsieur le Duc ever did, servants in livery, gold plate on the table . . ."

"And what's all that to you? It isn't your business."

"François, you, a clever, an intelligent man can say that —not my business! Whose business is it then?"

Lemot's clenched hands shot up. "Topino! You took an oath! You swore you'd leave politics alone, you swore you'd keep strictly to your work. You'd let the past die. You said you'd forget the whole thing . . ."

"François . . ." Topino smiled wanly. "I thought I could. But you see. . ." He took a deep breath. "One thinks one can give such a promise, but hold to it, one can't."

"My God, why not? You've been painting like you never have, Gracchus at Marseilles, now Orestes, it's the sensation of the Salon . . ."

"Sensation?"

"But of course!"

"History they call it. They say it's good history." Topino grinned. "That's how people look at art."

"What if they do? If they like it that way, let them.

You make a living, you're able to do what you love most and . . ."

"Oh don't, don't . . ." Topino was pacing the room, throwing his head back one moment, sending Lemot a pleading look the next. "I tried. I tried my best, I really did, but—" He shook his head. "A man can't tear out his heart, strip away everything he believes in. I can't shut my eyes to what's happening, people going mad over everything in uniform, carried away by fox tails dangling from helmets, cheering Bonaparte for taking their sons, for taking their freedom too, mangling the press, abolishing the vote, while his friends fatten on the money he steals from every country he overruns—"

"—while you go on dreaming of another Bastille day and let yourself be seen with Arena. Don't deny it!"

"I was never near the Opera. I've done nothing they can hold out against me, I haven't written pamphlets, I didn't speak in the streets . . ."

"You've drawn attention to yourself. That's enough in times like these. Your paintings, your subjects—why in hell would you want to paint someone like Gracchus? And what about the famous caricature, the one that looks so much like a certain gentleman?"

"Now really? Who would believe that." He laughed.

"You think that's something so funny? Duval's sure he recognizes himself. To set a man like Duval against you. . ."

"So Duval thinks my little sketch looks like him?" Topino almost doubled up with laughter.

[117]

Lemot's fists tightened. "Man, don't you see a thing like that can be suicidal?"

Topino's gaiety vanished. "I didn't think I was drawing anyone in particular."

"You can be sure he's had his eye on you ever since. As I get it," Lemot's voice sank to a whisper, "He has the police looking for the person who took delivery of the pistols. They've tracked down the gunsmith, they've made him talk."

Topino turned to his easel. Suddenly he looked like a man crushed, so bowed that Lemot had to come up very close to see his face.

"Thank God. You're finally beginning to see how things stand, why something has to be done. Today! Now! Right now!"

"They aren't going to uncover *one* thing against me."

"Let's hope you're right, but you can be pretty sure they'll find whatever they want to find. We can't wait till that happens. That's why I've been so busy this morning. I think I've got it fixed now so you'll be safe out of it."

"You? How could you . . . ?"

"I'm not for having you end up at the guillotine, so I've started things. You're a recognized artist. That counts; but better yet, you were a pupil of David's. David is Bonaparte's spoiled child. You're going to join the new painters' guild David is heading. Nothing could be more natural for an artist to do than join up with his former master."

"You mean you'd have me go along with a crowd like that, slaves willing to spend their time licking Bonaparte's boots?"

"Don't talk like that. You have no right to. David is a great man, a great painter. You'd be the last to deny it."

"I don't deny he *was.*"

"Was?"

"Yes, was. He *was* great. He got us away from all these boudoir scenes, those silly bergerettes; he gave the world something to think about. I can still see people standing there crying before his Oath of the Horatii. Yes, I say David was a very great man—before he became a turncoat. . . ."

"I tell you, you mustn't say that."

". . . before he began to paint generals brandishing flags, eyes raised to heaven, but never a glance for the dead who litter the ground."

"You were his pupil!"

"Yes, I was. And I thought the world of him. He was a leader, a revolutionary in every sense. But now? David, the old Jacobin, shudders at the word. For him I am just that —a Jacobin."

"However that is, he says he'll take you. He says he'll do anything we ask him to do."

"We? You say we?"

"Don't be naïve—a thing like this can't be managed without some inside help. Now get it into your head—you're going to join the guild. Cambacérès has agreed to back you. This afternoon I'll be coming back with Massat, the secretary of the guild. He'll interview you—just a formality. It has to be done though, so please tidy up the room a little, get into some decent clothes and—"

"Now? Not this afternoon."

[119]

"Are you out of your mind? Every minute counts. And for heaven's sake, be careful when he's talking to you, watch your words, be polite and try to be a little respectful. He won't make it hard, he'll be doing his best to help. All right now. Stop worrying. Once in the guild you'll be as safe as if you were Bonaparte's particular crony."

With that, Lemot began to slip into his coat, but Topino caught him by the arm. "Wait. I have to think this over."

Lemot turned to him, his face a mask. "You haven't time to think over anything."

"François, there has to be some other way."

"My God." Lemot spat out the words. "I tell you, you're as good as under arrest right now. What you have to do is wait till we get here and then be a little reasonable. Promise me you will be." With that Lemot loosened Topino's grip, but before he could reach the door Topino had stopped him again.

"Where're you going?"

"You ask?" Lemot stood there staring at him. "I'll be back here with Massat. Remember the name. And tidy up, please."

By the time he had finished, Topino had got between him and the door. "Wait—you are sure it's really that bad?"

Lemot looked at him in bewilderment. "For God's sake, pull yourself together."

Topino stood back. "All right. I'll do whatever you say."

"You mean it? You do, don't you?"

"Yes. I'll do whatever you say. Not for my own sake, though." While Lemot choked back the question—for whose sake then?—Topino's eyes went down to his feet.

[120]

"Most of the time it's . . . it's as if it didn't matter one way or the other, as if life weren't worth that much." And then taking Lemot by the hand, "Thank you, François," he said. "Thank you for your friendship, for giving me back some of my faith in the world, in humanity. Believe me that's worth more than a lot of things, more than—being saved."

Lemot smiled. "Don't forget," he said as he started down the stairs, "it's a formality. Nothing more."

Going down, Lemot was so deep in thought he failed to notice the greasy handrail, the filthy walls, the rubbish piled at every landing, which would ordinarily have repelled a man as accustomed to good living as he was. In the street, he paused for a moment, drawing in the humid autumn air. *"Ouf."* He looked back at the tall, narrow building he had just left and then across the street to the beautiful town house opposite, built not so many years back by the Duc de Luynes whose name remained stubbornly attached to it. Duval must have had the façade done over. It stood out now like a dandy among the rabble of the streets.

The fiacre he had come in was still there at the curb and already the driver was holding the door open, but Lemot waved him away. A walk would do him good, give him a chance to think things through. Besides, it took no time really to get to the Luxembourg.

The silence in these side streets was restoring him already. He looked up. The sky was streaked with silver. His artist's eye lingered on the delicate shading, the gray formations' rhythmic harmonies, the soft blue patches between, which stood out like promises of eternity against the drab reality of

[121]

the buildings. How Paris had changed! Yes, even here between the river and St. Germain-des-Prés, how different things were from what they had been, say ten years back, when he had lived here himself. In the Rue de Tournon he passed the Hotel de Nivernais where he had worked so many years ago carving the fountain at the garden entrance. The place was hardly recognizable now that they'd cut it up to make apartments, its façade leprous, besmirched, and still carrying the marks of the bad years, the slogans scrawled in the hideous brown of discolored blood, *"Liberté, fraternité ou la mort."*

And like Paris the world had changed too, with everyone forced to make the kind of adjustments Topino, for reasons not apparent, seemed unwilling or unable to make. What was the demon that kept his mind so hopelessly entangled with what had passed. Topino was an intelligent man, a brave man. Why couldn't he change too?

Looking back on the talk they'd just had, he could see so many things about the man that defied explanation. Why, after all he had been through, would he wilfully involve himself in a scheme as crazy as Arena's, which might, supposing it had come off, have plunged the country into something very much like civil war? Again, what would induce him to break the promises he had given, and most of all— what was it in the man that made him act so consistently in ways opposed to his own best interests?

In his mind Lemot tried to see his friend as he had been back in those early days of the Revolution when for some months they had shared a room here in this very quarter. At that time he had thought he knew Topino well, and yet, what can one ever know really about some other person? Before the first stages of the Revolution passed, their ways had parted; for a couple of years they completely lost track of each other, and it was only during the last terrible days of the Terror, when everyone who was not a Jacobin of Jacobins was being rounded up or in fear of being rounded up, that they encountered each other again. Lemot remembered the moment well. He was in deep trouble, wanted by the police, and as a hunted man it was a happy surprise to discover that Topino in some way had influence with those in power. In only a matter of hours the charges had been dropped.

It was at this same time too that he learned of the strides Topino had been making in his work. The Revolution had given him his chance as it had so many others, but unlike the myriad of adventurers, rascals, daredevils who had come to the fore and then been swallowed up by the same tide that had exalted them, he had succeeded in making a place for himself in those art circles that counted most. What distinguished him from most of his fellows there was the enthusiasm and devotion he felt for the democratic cause. Ever since the beginning he had been fired by Robespierre and Robespierre's puritanism, but inevitably a day came when his humanity put him at odds with that implacable man, and Topino found himself in his own cell in the Temple. Only with Robespierre's fall had Topino been released, but from then on the two friends did see each other from time to time.

These were the first days of the Directory when so many of one's hours were spent in the cafés around the Palais Royal. The new regime, corrupt beyond belief, had revolted both of them, but Lemot, going in his mind over those days, recalled how careful he had been to mask his feelings and concentrate on work. Topino, on the other hand, was soon playing at Revolution again. Along with a few other die-hard Jacobins he had joined in the movement of Babeuf—"Gracchus" Babeuf, as he liked to be called. In a very short time he had become one of the man's principal followers, and after Babeuf's arrest, conviction and suicide in 1797 it was something of a miracle that Topino escaped with a sentence of exile and nothing more. Under guard, he had been escorted across the Swiss frontier, and as Topino told it afterwards, the following three years in Switzerland had been an agony. Too depressed to paint he had let himself vegetate, and when in its turn the Directory went under and he was allowed to return to Paris, he found his old haunts in the Rue Jacob next thing to paradise. He had thrown himself into his work with a concentration so total that what he produced was above anything he had done before. No doubt for the first time in years life must have seemed beautiful, and then one day something—who could say what?—had started him off again.

This much was clear though. He saw Bonaparte and his new order as pure tyranny, the negation of everything the Revolution had struggled for, and perhaps it was too much to expect any other reaction from one with Topino's heart and character. But even so, considering his terrible experiences in the past, considering the success he was now having, it was paradoxical that he should suddenly risk everything, all the promise that life now held for him.

Lemot looked up. There ahead he could see the flattened

gables of the Luxembourg. Massat would be waiting at the side entrance—stout fellow, Massat, coming forward to help a man he had never seen, and doing so out of nothing more than the goodness of his heart. Lemot slowed his pace. Conscious suddenly of all that the next hour might bring, his mind came back with even more concern to the peril Topino was in. "Not directly implicated." Did he really imagine a plea like that would be enough? Had he ever taken the trouble to give thought to Bonaparte's own position?

Quite evidently Topino never had. Not once had he bothered to ask himself what a dictator must do to consolidate the power he had seized only months before. To be sure, the 18th of Brumaire had made Bonaparte First Consul, and the victory of Marengo had practically delivered the country to him; but even so, in spite of his genius he was still the *arriviste* in the eyes of many, a novice as chief of state who had still to prove himself. What was more natural than that his first moves should be directed against what opposition remained, and that the means used should be precisely those men in his case were traditionally forced to use? Bonaparte was a man who had learned the lessons of history. His approach to his adversaries, the extremists on either hand, Jacobin or Royalist, was the classic two-pronged maneuver —favors showered on those willing to conform and threats for everyone else.

For heaven's sake, then, if Topino had to consider Bonaparte his personal enemy, why didn't he study the man a little before taking to arms? Bonaparte's handling of the situation was perfectly clear.

Deep in thought, Lemot continued his way along the

length of the Rue de Seine, going back over the situation step by step. To begin with, Bonaparte had made every concession to the Royalists; he had encouraged the emigrés to return, and assigned the greatest names to high offices. With a Prince de Talleyrand-Perigord at the head of the foreign ministry, the old nobility could feel secure and whatever opposition remained in that camp could be placated sooner or later by bribery—money had to play a role in any dictator's scheming.

That the policy was working was apparent too. After only a few months the Royalists, save for a few hotheads, were a threat no longer, which left the Jacobins the one real danger. Here his strategy was proving as effective as with the Royalists. Fouché, a regicide, the butcher of Lyon, the hangman of the Loire, a man who had erected guillotines in every city of the South of France, had been installed as minister of police, an appointment which made it clear the First Consul held no grudge against former Jacobins as such—at least not so long as they were disposed to play along with him. At the same time, this charitable attitude was paralleled by a campaign of extermination not so different from the manhunts which had made the Revolution infamous. Ideologues were "vermin who were better drowned"; Bonaparte had said that and it was clear he would never rest until the last of them was gone. Just this past week a proclamation had gone forth forewarning the Parisians that examples would be made, that Fouché had his orders, and Fouché, as everyone knew, was a man who never hesitated to do what was expected of him. Arena and Ceracchi—what if they were only fumbling plotters who had not been able to put their plot into effect?

What difference would that make to a Fouché?

It was here Topino's danger lay. Fouché was looking for victims. He would stop at nothing to incriminate a Jacobin no matter what he was, assassin or mere dreamer. If necessary he would even concoct the needed evidence. Rumor had it that Fouché's agents had "arranged" the attempt at the Opera, that when it became evident the plotters were penniless they had seen to it that a gunsmith should be paid to provide them with weapons, even though the possession of pistols, a saber even, was a capital crime. The subsequent unfolding of events, the circumstances surrounding the gala at the Opera, all seemed a little too pat to be entirely genuine —Bonaparte's appearance according to a schedule carefully announced, the arrival of Eugène de Beauharnais and his chasseurs seconds before, the following search of everyone in the house for weapons—all showed the Fouché touch. Arena and Ceracchi had been sitting in the parterre. As soon as the pistols and daggers were found on them they had been carried off to jail, and with that disposed of, the curtain had gone up.

To anyone with even a faintly suspicious turn of mind all this suggested careful planning, the existence of a counter-plot which became even more plausible when one recalled that Arena, like Napoleon, was a Corsican, and Ceracchi, a Roman, who at least at one time had been rather close to the Bonapartes. Ten years back both of the accused had been living in Marseilles when the Bonapartes were settled there; they could hardly help knowing a little too much about the history of the family and particularly about Bonaparte's own now-almost-forgotten flirtation with the Jacobins. Anything relating to this last would hardly fit the First Consul's present design, that is, to present himself as a man above party, one who had never indulged in politics or been allied to any faction. It all added up to one conclusion: Arena and Ceracchi, probably for weeks back, had been marked for liquidation. Sending them to their deaths would certainly intimidate such political clubs as still existed and silence those few die-hards who still clung to the old ideals, still dared to speak of liberty. And to these last Topino obviously belonged.

Thank God for Massat. Good old Massat! There he was on the sidewalk, just ahead, waiting, waiting to do his part. By now he would have had it out with Cambacérès, and Cambacérès was hardly one to make difficulties. Recently installed as Second Consul, minister of justice as well, he was the perfect example of the parvenu, a man obsessed by only two desires: first, to fill his pockets, and then to get a toehold in the quartier St. Germain. Naturally Cambacérès would be only too pleased to do anything he might to obligate an old aristocrat like Count Massat, and that being so, Topino's case was in good hands. A few minutes' tactful interview with Topino, a yes following from Cambacérès, and even Fouché would be helpless.

By this time Massat had caught sight of Lemot and was beckoning him on.

"It's taken you a devilishly long time, my friend," he said, hustling Lemot into the cab he had waiting. "What they're saying inside there about what's coming," he nodded toward the palace, "makes me think we'd do well to hurry."

As they went rattling off, he proceeded to bring Lemot up to date. Everything considered, things looked reasonably good. Cambacérès had done the necessary and David was ready to cooperate. The great painter had said yes, yes indeed, he liked Topino-Lebrun very much, he liked his work and would be glad to have him in the guild. You could only say David had shown himself at his kindest, but apart from that—and here was the bad news—Fouché was apparently out to show his boss he could anticipate his intentions; word was that he planned to have all the conspirators locked up by nightfall.

"Was there any specific mention of our friend?" Lemot was trying hard to remain composed.

"I'm afraid there was, but if all goes well—and why shouldn't it?—Monsieur Lebrun should be as safe by that time as if he were a consul himself."

With that, Massat gave his friend a pat on the shoulder and started to talk about what had happened last night at Mme. Tallien's little palace in the Rue Babylone, Mme. Tallien—Notre Dame de Thermidor, as some wits liked to call her. His cheerfulness communicated so well that by the time they were climbing the creaking stairs to Topino's, both were laughing and joking, among other things about the accumulations of dirt that greeted you no matter where you looked, one accomplishment of the Revolution, they both agreed, which no observer could possibly deny.

Walking into the studio, they found Topino deep in his work, absorbed completely. He was still in the same clothes, the room as untidy as before. Lemot's reproachful look only drew a helpless gesture. He was sorry—Topino nodded toward his canvas—he had been trying to get these last details right while the paint was still wet.

Lemot could only make the best of it and proceed with the introductions, giving them a touch of the comical with a series of exaggerated bows first to one, then the other.

"My dear Massat, let me present my famous friend Topino-Lebrun, creator of such masterworks as The *Death of Gracchus* and *Orestes and The Furies,* which I'm sure you've heard about or seen at the Salon." And then to Topino, "I want you to meet Camille Massat, not a dealer, not a buyer, but in fact something far better, a friend."

"Monsieur." Smiling broadly Massat made a sweeping bow.

There was a pause. Then, with a pointed *"citoyen"* and a not-too-gracious wave of the hand, Topino bade his guests be seated. "Forgive me if things here aren't as comfortable as you're probably used to having them."

There was a second's chill, which passed quickly as Massat, with a laugh, proceeded to clear the papers out of a chair. Everything here, he announced, was quite to his liking and he was only hoping—this with a good-natured little bow— that he could make this visit as short as possible so it would not interfere with Monsieur's work, work necessarily more important than any talk he could imagine the two of them having. In due time he would like to ask the few questions he was obliged to ask, but before coming to that he wanted to say how honored he was to meet an artist whose imagination one couldn't help admiring.

This struck Lemot as a wonderfully subtle way of beginning such an interview, and to help things along he added that he himself had wondered many times what it could be that provided the inspiration for so many unusual subjects.

Massat seized on this. "Could it possibly have something to do with your having lived out of the country? You were in Switzerland for a time, I recall. Mountains such as those would surely set thoughts stirring in an artist's mind."

"It's my hope I never see them again."

"So . . .? But, if I'm not mistaken, you were there for something like three years."

"Two years, six months and fifteen days. The government at the moment, the so-called Directory, considered my presence in France as an unnecessary hazard, a hazard that is to their private well-being."

"Not really." Massat did his best to make his laugh seem natural. "The way you put it! Well, Monsieur, it *is* good to be in one's homeland, isn't it, to breathe our Paris air, however smoky. I know, because as it happens, I was an emigré myself and forced to spend a certain amount of time abroad."

"I rather doubt the circumstances were exactly comparable." Topino was making no effort to hide his sarcasm. "In certain ways, though, you are more fortunate than I. As an emigré you returned to find things very much to your taste, I would guess, while I came back to find Bonaparte so busy restoring things it was almost as if we had Louis XVI with us again."

Lemot decided it was time to put a stop to this.

"I think you know, Topino, what it is we're here about. I'm sure you realize events are making the air of Paris unhealthy for you again, and since we would all like to see you remain and go on working undisturbed, the painters' guild has proposed a way to smooth things over, an agreeable, I

[131]

might even say, an elegant way."

"Nothing could be simpler," Massat threw in with a courteous smile. "All it requires is a commitment on your part, an almost innocuous commitment by which you—"

"Pardon, Massat," Lemot cut in. "I think I can explain it to our friend. Massat here represents the guild, the guild every painter worth his salt is wishing he could join, which—"

"I didn't realize—you are a painter, *citoyen?*"

Lemot gave Massat a sign to let him go on with the talking.

"No, Massat is not a painter," he said with as much good-nature as he could muster, "but he is in good standing with the government, and the government's consent must be had for each new admission. Massat is ready to get that for you. Both he and I feel it'll prove a very pleasant experience for you, a chance to work in peace and with David, your old instructor."

"Pleasant?" There was a short laugh. "It'll be instructive, all right. He's probably the best example we've had of how one adapts to the practical requirements of the times."

Massat coughed. "Interesting. Very interesting, but if you'll forgive me, we might do well to push on. Suppose I take a few things down. Pure formality, you know," and getting out his notebook, he went on: "You worked with David. Can you tell me when and for how long? You know what sticklers people can be sometimes about certain trivialities these last turbulent years."

"I was with David until I gave up painting."

As he said this Topino went back to his easel and picked

up palette and brushes. It was as if he were saying this was the end of the interview.

"Gave up painting? You mean you actually stopped painting?" Massat's astonishment was genuine. "Is that possible for an artist? You mean to say you—"

"It was a time when the country needed men more than it needed painters."

A pause followed during which nothing was to be heard but Topino's knife scraping at the dry paint. Presently Massat managed a laugh.

"Quite so. Quite so," he said. "I can well see it. You were like so many. You did what you thought one had to do for the country. You served in the way you thought best, even though it turned out in the end to be something less perhaps than the very best way."

"You refer to the events of the year Two, I take it."

"Couldn't we call it 1794? It makes everything so much easier. And I do hope you'll excuse me if I try to get on with this report. Just another question or two. It's been said you served under Robespierre. Served is probably a very imprecise term, but however that is, it's well known your intervention did soften many of Robespierre's decisions, moved him toward leniency."

"You'd like to know what my function was, just how I served; that's what you need for your report, is it?"

Before Massat could say anything Lemot had intervened.

"Painter. Put down painter. Topino's always been a painter, whatever he says," and to Topino, "Massat isn't in the least interested in anything else you might have done. Besides, can anyone say exactly what he was doing that many years ago, nearly six, isn't it, especially after the kind of years we've been going through since."

"How right you are." Massat sent Lemot a glance of gratitude. "Weren't we all up to our necks in things we'd just as soon not be reminded of? I know all too well, I was certainly no exception. Well then. I'll put down painter. Pupil of David. Adviser of the government on the restoration and decoration of public buildings. That *is* correct, is it not?" he added, turning to Topino.

"Very kind of you to describe me that way." Topino faced Massat. "But forgive me. To what do I owe all this . . . I mean this solicitude on your part?"

"You really don't know?"

Topino looked at him blankly.

"The name Massat conveys nothing? Rings no bell?" and as Topino's eyebrows went up, "Doesn't it recall a scene in court and a Massat being sentenced to die?"

"Count Massat? Yes. Yes, I do remember. I remember very well. But that wasn't you."

"No. It was my father. The others went to the guillotine, but not he, and he always said it was you who saved him. How you were able to do it he never did say, but I'm sure it took an act of heroism on your part. Now that he's dead I often wonder how it was possible for you to get him out of Robespierre's clutches."

Again Lemot broke in.

"It's very simple, Massat. Robespierre liked Topino. Topino was close to Robespierre and so . . ."

"No," Topino cut in harshly. "It was not because I was a friend of Robespierre. I could do what I did because I was

[134]

a member of the Tribunal Revolutionnaire."

A moment of stunned silence followed. Lemot dropped into a chair and sat there staring ahead, while Massat, after a long pause, went on in a voice so choked it was almost inaudible. "You . . . you were—you . . ."

Topino looked at him. "Go on. Why don't you say it?"

". . . you were one of them, Fouquier-Tinville's gang of butchers?" As Topino turned away, Massat's eyes searched Lemot's with the silent question: "Did *you* know that?"

It helped Lemot get control of himself.

"I can assure you this much, Massat. In that position Topino was able to do a great deal of good."

"I was a juror." Topino's voice was cold, factual, almost indifferent. "I voted with the rest, for or against; many times for, a few times against."

"A juror!" Massat was still trying to take it in. "In Fouquier-Tinville's court? You, a decent man, a sensitive man, an artist . . ."

Topino shrugged, and in a stereotyped gesture began scraping at his palette while Lemot answered for him.

"Don't forget this, Massat. David's workshop was the gathering place for all the hotheads, a breeding ground for every crazy idea. All the young ones were bitten by it. Everyone of them thought he had to be in it, but if you need proof Topino was not in love with the tribunal and its way, remember how soon he was under suspicion himself, how soon they packed him off to prison like the rest. His sense of decency, his sense of justice almost cost him his life."

Massat got up and went over to Topino.

"I shouldn't have said what I said. Forgive me." He offered a hand which Topino either didn't see or didn't care to see. "You saved my father's life, and you risked your own doing it. I never forgot the name of the man to whom I owed this, and now that I've met that man and know the risk he took I never will forget him, not to the end of my days." He clasped his hands together.

"I helped send many a one to the guillotine." Head down, Topino walked the room up and down, up and down, his visitors following him with their eyes, doing their best to hide the sense of awe that had come over them. "You wonder how it's possible to do that? It's simple, really. You believe you have to. I know I did. I thought everyone had to do his part, end what was ruining France—rule by incompetents, degenerates, scoundrels—end the injustice, the dishonesty, make a clean sweep of it, clean it out completely, every last bit, the whole thing! You couldn't make decent bread with moldy dough, that was how the reasoning went."

Lemot had recovered by this time.

"Oh, come . . . let the past die, let it bury itself. Massat doesn't care what you thought or did. The one thing that matters for him is that you worked in David's workshop."

Massat sat down and opened his book. He was still shaken but making a brave effort to hide his feelings, present a show of understanding, use the proper conciliatory words.

"You make a good point," he said. "You put it very clearly. What it really comes down to is the theory of revolution, and from that point of view I can well see how certain acts we condemn now would have appeared defensible then."

"You are most kind."

Massat shifted in his chair. "I want you to know I appreciate your frankness, and I will say that whatever my personal opinion happens to be it is still good to have these reports of how it all ended for you. I don't know what stronger proof one could ask than the fact that when Robespierre and the other members of the Tribunal went to the scaffold you were released."

Topino shrugged. "I had friends, artists who . . .".

Lemot was quick to cut this off. "No. You broke with Robespierre, you made it plain to everybody you weren't up to what he was expecting of you, but even if this isn't enough for certain people, even if some still call you a Jacobin, how old were you? Twenty-four? A youngster fired by every tale he heard about court scandals, diamond necklaces . . ."

"No, François. You can't blame it on youth. With me it was no passing phase. I still—"

"Please, messieurs." Nervously Massat riffled his notes. "It was never my intention to be indiscreet. All I was hoping to get was some reassurance as to your present attitudes, and I trust you won't misunderstand if I ask you to confirm what I'm about to say. Now, if you will, please listen carefully and tell me if I have it right."

"Well?"

"After Thermidor you settled down with your work until Babeuf came along. That's correct, isn't it?"

"That's correct."

"Babeuf created a great stir and you, like many people who had no faith in the Directory, found yourself caught up in it. Now I must say it's hard for a person like myself to understand anyone's feeling he could support a creature like

[137]

Babeuf, but I'm sure you didn't share his more extreme ideas."

"Up to a point I . . ."

"Well, anyway, you found yourself exiled and only came home when you saw the country had come to its senses, come back to law and order." Massat was looking Topino straight in the face. "I'm sure you agree that this has been accomplished now." And when no answer came: "Or at least that the ideals of the Revolution are by way of being realized, realized in practical terms—that we're beginning to have the kind of equality people like yourself have always dreamed of."

"Equality?" Topino laughed. "Bonaparte's equality, you mean. Maybe I should tell you what he said to one of his officers when he tried to protest. I'm quoting. You still believe in liberty and equality? It's easy to see you're the son of a bricklayer. That's what Bonaparte said and that's Bonaparte's idea of equality for you."

Massat rose. "Monsieur, tales like that—they're simply slanders, they're simply not true!"

"Well then, come over here. Please. Have a look at that house there across the street. My neighbor is a great man, a rich man. He had a ball last night. Look, some of the guests are just leaving now. See the coaches, the ribbons, the jewels? Lovely, aren't they? In less than two years my neighbor's made a fortune a duke would have been proud to have even in the old days. In fact, except for his manners, which are not quite what they might be, Monsieur Duval"—he emphasized the word Monsieur—"is another Monsieur le Duc all over again."

[138]

Massat shrugged and went back to his chair. "Be a little patient, *mon cher*. Bonaparte will be rid of him and his likes in a matter of months."

"You think so? Bonaparte's more likely to make sure his regime is profitable to any scoundrel who'll back him."

This was more than Massat could swallow. "Order, that's what we need," he almost shouted. "Order, not sentiment! Order and peace! Bonaparte's seeing to it we have both."

"Peace? He? Oh yes. Oh yes indeed. He'll give us peace just the way he's given us peace before—through war. And order? What better way to get order than to kill off everyone who doesn't cheer? Bonaparte's nothing but another Robespierre on horseback."

"Mind what you're saying, Monsieur!"

With that, Massat started forward, eyes ablaze, but in an instant Lemot was between them.

"Massat, please! Topino's only saying what we all know. A million things need doing, a million things aren't right yet."

"All right." Massat went back to his chair biting his lips, sat down and began to write. "I'll say nothing about Monsieur's political leanings. I'll put down that as an artist he's interested in art and nothing else. And by the way, Monsieur"—Massat looked up—"art has great days ahead." There was a glow of pride in his eyes. "You may be one of the lucky ones. Bonaparte's giving commissions every day to men like you. He's a great admirer of David. Your turn should come."

"Very possibly. Bonaparte knows how to reward his toadies."

Before Massat could react, Lemot was speaking, his voice almost pleading.

"Listen to what Massat's telling you. It's true. Bonaparte's giving us our chances. Take me. He's proposing me for the Institute. He wants me to do the carvings for—some monument he's planning for the Carrousel. He's for encouraging any artist who has ideas—"

". . . that please him."

"Monsieur," Massat's voice was almost strident now. "What we know is that Bonaparte's bringing happiness back to this country."

"Is he now? My best hope for you, *citoyen,* is that you survive the kind of happiness he brings."

This was too much. Between furious glances Massat started scribbling frantically at his notes.

"Monsieur, I'm *most* grateful to you for your *most* honest answers. I'm glad I can put down that you're a *devoted* partisan of the new order but that in spite of that fact, in spite of your admiration for its principles, you feel you must put art *first*—you follow me?—I mean that it's your intention to devote yourself to your painting full time and—and *exclusively.*" Glaring at Topino, he added, "Is that correct?"

Topino folded his arms. "And what more?"

"More?" There was a short laugh. "That you have courage." Clapping his notebook shut, he reached for his hat. "I'll be back shortly. With your certificate of membership, I hope. I've the strong impression, Monsieur, you're going to need it."

With that he was off, slamming the door behind him.

[140]

For a minute both stood motionless, Topino half-turned away, both listening as the footsteps faded. Then, as if awakening from some nightmare, Topino picked up his palette and started mixing paint.

Lemot went back to his chair and for a time sat there staring ahead, mechanically following Topino's movements. Finally, in a low voice, he broke the silence.

"Was it really necessary to carry on like that—after my begging you, begging you so sincerely to be a little reasonable, after begging you to act like a reasonable man?"

"I'm sorry, François, but . . . but all that talk, Bonaparte's loving the common man—I just couldn't take it."

"What now, then? What can we expect? He's outraged, furious. Is he going to go out of his way to save a man who sneers at everything he believes in? He said he'd be back, but will he?"

"I'm sorry. I couldn't stomach one more of his platitudes."

"Even so you should have kept your mouth shut. God Almighty, you certainly should—if only for *my* sake. Can't you imagine the time I had getting him here, one of the old regime to the house of a Jacobin?"

"Of course you're right, François. I was stupid. You've done everything you can; too much, even. You'd better go now. You mustn't be seen here, now less than ever. Thanks, though. Thanks for everything." Having said it, he sat down at the easel and began to concentrate on his work as if there were no one else in the room.

For a time Lemot watched him.

"You know, when I look at you I don't know what to

think. Even now you don't realize what's hanging over you."

"Oh, I'm not that dull. Massat is probably telling the police right now every word I said."

"Never believe it. Massat's a gentleman. If I know him, he'll be back in the hour with your appointment, and you'll be saved in spite of your crazy, your unbelievable performance. But mind you. You're going to have to change, just as he was saying. And there's another thing I have to tell you: you're going to have to change the things you paint, your subjects."

"My subjects? What's wrong with them?"

"My God, they're provocative, challenging! *The Death of Gracchus!* The name's bad enough. It brings back all kinds of things, not just Roman tribunes, but Babeuf and all that; it's as if you were defending him, mourning him. And now this *Orestes.* People stand there, staring, shuddering inside. It makes them uncomfortable, self-conscious."

"Orestes avenging his father? Myths like that are legitimate subjects, aren't they?"

"But that's not what you painted! You haven't painted his vengeance! You've painted him fleeing, pursued by the Furies. The Furies are about to take vengeance on *him!* The horror that conjures up!"

"Do you think a man can kill without any feeling of remorse?"

"No, but even so—to present it that way, to show a man tortured, hunted down—I tell you, in times like these, . . . Topino, you should understand this—anything about killing or having killed is something you shouldn't touch. Or talk about, much less paint. The thing's taboo. Once and for all, you have to give up these things, come up with something pleasant, something—well, intimate. Haven't you got anything like that?"

"Intimate?" Topino managed a smile. "You think intimate things are more apt to be pleasant?—No! Don't! Not that one! Please!"

Lemot had gone over to an easel in a corner of the workshop and was about to remove the cloth that covered it.

"Don't! Don't!" Topino shouted.

"Don't get so excited. I'm not going to look if you don't want me to. Honest to God, Topino, I can't make you out, and I'm not just talking about your *Orestes* or what's happened today. I don't think I ever could have understood you. Someday you're going to have to tell me, man to man . . ." He stopped.

"Tell you what?"

Lemot gave him a hard look. "Well, what really made you get into this mess."

"So. You don't understand. I look a little strange to you. You want to know what it is about me that. . . . All right. You want to know." Topino went over to the covered easel. "This may explain some of it."

He took the cloth away and Lemot gasped. There, in grisly detail, was shown a group of severed heads.

"Heads . . . blood . . ." Lemot couldn't get the words out clearly. "You . . . you *painted* them . . . you sat there and . . ."

"I'd never have shown you this, but you wanted to know. You wanted to know about me."

"The guillotine! You mean you . . . you . . ."

"I saw every one of them. Alive." Topino nodded toward the painting. "You could say I knew all of them. I saw them file out on their way to the tumbrel. This one"—he pointed to a head in the foreground—"you see him, how innocent he looked; he didn't seem to understand what was happening, he had the face of a child really. And the one next. He was composure itself, he said nothing, offered no defense, just looked at us with contempt; you couldn't help admiring him. And then the one behind, there; he ignored us, acted as if he didn't see us, as if he didn't hear what was being said, and we couldn't help feeling humiliated. But worse than any of these, worst of all, was number four, over there. He begged, he pleaded. Not for his life. He wanted to die in secret so his wife and children wouldn't see or know."

"Please. That's enough of it. Please!"

"And the last one there in the background. He said 'Thank you' and bowed as he left, like a guest leaving a party. You said something about forgetting. You think one forgets a face like that?"

"And you painted them."

"Yes, I did."

"But why? Why?"

"Those faces are with me always, day and night. Painting them . . . well, it relieves you a bit."

"My God. You and Orestes . . . now I see why people are always finding a likeness between you and the man in your painting. The Furies? You know an awful lot about them, don't you."

Topino stood there shaking his head. "We all thought we were doing the right thing, everyone of us on the tribunal, but even so, even so. . . . There's something about sending a man to his death, even if you're doing it in the best of faith, something—I can't say what it is—it isn't easy to explain. It seems to me, François, it seems that every one of us has to pay his due, sooner or later."

While he was speaking Topino had been covering the picture again. The loud voices in the street hadn't got through to him, but Lemot was at the window.

"Police, Topino. They're questioning everybody. They've got that girl of yours right now."

"What!" Topino was at his side. "Police? You're sure? They don't look like—"

"Of course they're police. Wait. Where are you going?"

Topino was already out of the room. Lemot followed as far as the landing and watched while his friend raced down the stairs. Then, shaking his head, he went back into the studio.

Topino came out into the street just as the men there were turning from Mariette to her mother. Taking advantage of the moment, he caught the girl by the arm and pulled her back into the little inner courtyard.

"What is it? What did they want to know?"

"Just what they were asking before. The gunsmith, did I know him."

"And what did you say?"

She laughed. "That I didn't know there was a gunsmith in the quartier."

"And then?"

"Nothing. They just looked at me and went on to mother and the others. Had anyone seen a woman get a package at the gunsmith's? It seems the gunsmith told them it was a woman who took it."

Topino's fists came up against his forehead. "Never. I never should have. I shouldn't have asked you. But you're sure, absolutely sure no one saw you?"

"I told you. No one. I've told you that again and again! No one could have seen me. It was pouring rain, a regular cloudburst. The street was as empty as my hand. There wasn't a soul in sight and I was back in no time."

"I never, never should have asked you, but . . . how else . . . they were watching me, time was running out and . . . Swear it, Mariette. Swear whatever they do you'll say you don't know me."

"But how could I?"

"Say I'm just another of the men whose rooms you take care of. Careful." Mariette's mother had appeared in the courtyard entrance. "Careful. You don't know me."

With that he hurried upstairs again.

At the upper landing he stopped. Voices were coming from his room. He stood listening for a second, then threw the door open. A familiar figure was sitting there chatting with Lemot. As Topino closed the door, the visitor got up, bowed and smiled.

"Yes, you're quite right. Duval. I'm glad you recognize me. We never have met really—glanced at each other would be more like it, I daresay—but suppose we let this make up for all the other times."

Topino's eyes ran over him from head to foot. The man seemed badly out of place in these surroundings. The bulky figure, florid cheeks, his look of prosperity and air of dignity, all clashed with the squalor, the disorder of the room. Goodwill as well as self-satisfaction radiated from him. Somehow he had the look of a man who feels himself above the troubles of this world, one eager to sweep trouble away no matter where he finds it. He was dressed with great care. The double-breasted vest of white piqué, the broad jabot that swathed his neck and came almost to his ears, the satiny coat that nearly swept the floor and the bottines reaching halfway up the calf, all suggested a man of fashion rather than the entrepreneur, the sort of fop you might see strolling in the gardens of the Palais Royal rather than a man on the Exchange.

Topino's continuing silence apparently disturbed him not at all.

"My dear Monsieur Lebrun, we were just having a friendly little chat, Monsieur Lemot and I"—he seemed to be listening with pleasure to his own words—"a chat about you, as a matter of fact, how we could best help you in this . . . eh, rather thorny situation you find yourself in. Now that we're together, the three of us, it should be easy to come to an understanding." He came forward a step or two, obviously with the intention of offering his hand, but when Topino made no corresponding move he good-naturedly turned back to his chair. "Before we get into that, let me assure you, it is a real pleasure, a real honor, to meet my famous neighbor in person."

"I can't imagine what you and I could have to say to each other." Topino turned to the door as if to open it for him.

"Please. A chat, just a friendly chat. Friendly I say, because even if you find it hard to believe, I am your friend.

Sit down. Be patient. You misjudge me, Monsieur Lebrun. You have a completely wrong conception of me. I have nothing against you. No sir, not a thing. As a matter of fact, I rather like you. I like your courage, your sincerity, and I can understand your opinions, even your aversion, say, yes, even the dislike you almost certainly have for someone of my kind, and though it may seem paradoxical, I can't say I altogether blame you."

"Shall we get to the point? What is it you want of me?"

"Oh come now . . ." With a smile Duval turned to Lemot. "I'm beginning to believe he's every bit the hothead you said he was. Here I am, coming to see him with the best intentions, hoping we'll be able to smooth out all our little differences, and how does he react? Very nearly turns me out, and why?"—he was still addressing this to Lemot—"Because he mistrusts me, sees me as a symbol of the world he rejects, because it grieves him to see an order of things reestablished which may be too much, too disciplined for him to adapt to."

"That's out-and-out slander!"

"You think that isn't the reason? Wouldn't you agree, Monsieur Lemot, a furious denial, that's about all we get from these idealists? They set out to build a society with softer rules, a society based on love and fraternity, where life is easy, a paradise for all—a childish dream, but a beautiful dream, a dream I feel for. But what happens? They simply won't concede that it doesn't work, and that's why men like Lebrun here are so difficult. I can understand them, I can even understand them very well; but the thing I deplore is their inability to be a little understanding toward men like me."

[148]

"Forgive me, *Citoyen* Duval. We understand you very well. Too well for your own good."

Ignoring this, Duval went straight on, his eyes never leaving Lemot. "Take men like myself. We adjust to rules. We accept the world as it is, we don't try to bargain with the hard school that deals with the realities of human nature. What we acquire is the result of hard work, hard thinking. I'm one who's been able to do this, and at the same time help rebuild society from near-chaos. Is it unreasonable that I want to see my work safeguarded? Is it unreasonable I want to be able to continue to work in a quiet, orderly setting? Bonaparte makes this possible. He's recognized that the equality of Robespierre and Babeuf works out to be an idle dream. Being a sensible man, Bonaparte's trying to give people what they want most, a normal world in which they can live a normal life . . ."

". . . normal meaning unjust, quite naturally."

This time Duval turned to Topino. ". . . less unjust, my friend, less abominable than the injustices inflicted by those who set out to establish divine justice on earth."

"Maybe, but still just enough to have kept clever jackals from—"

Lemot jumped up. "Topino, please. Monsieur has something to propose. Let's listen to him."

Duval wasn't letting himself be silenced. "I was saying . . ." Coming halfway out of his chair, he let his voice rise as if addressing a room full of people. "I feel it's my right, nay, my duty, to neglect nothing I can do to protect myself, my world, against a crowd of utopians who once again would like to . . ."

[149]

The knocking at the door silenced him. When Lemot opened it, Massat walked in, and Duval, calming down, sank back into his chair and began smoothing his clothes back into their proper folds and creases.

"Thank God!" Lemot pulled out a chair. "I thought you were never coming. Sit down. Sit down."

Massat waved him away. His face was strained, it was plain that he was dead tired. From where he was standing he let his glance wander from one to the other until it finally came to rest on Duval, who promptly got to his feet again as Lemot began the introductions.

"Massat, you know M. Duval, I suppose. Monsieur Duval, this is Monsieur Massat, just come from the Luxembourg on some important business for us."

Duval made a little bow which went unanswered by Massat.

"Monsieur Duval . . . well, well." Looking around, Massat seemed to be trying to suppress a feeling of sardonic amusement. "The four of us, a rather disparate gathering, you might say, but a nice little company of friends all the same," and without giving the others a chance to interrupt he turned to Topino. "As I promised I did my best and it proved to be enough. The paper is on its way. Monsieur Cambacérès assured me there would be no opposition. He's not exactly an admirer of all your work, but he considers you worthy of the government's protection. So long as you're willing to go along with—"

"Forgive me, Monsieur," Duval broke in. "May I properly know what it is you're talking about?"

Still addressing Topino, Massat went on. "Monsieur Topino-Lebrun, on the assurance that you will observe all the association's rules, you are admitted to David's guild of painters, on the usual conditions and with all the usual privileges."

Duval sprang up. "How's that? You mean they're letting him remain here, here in Paris? He's allowed to go on producing this brand of—what he calls art?"

This time Massat did turn to Duval.

"Pardon, Monsieur. I thought I'd made that clear. There are conditions. You must have heard me. He's accepted on his promise to observe all guild rules, one being that every member submits for approval any subject he intends to paint."

Topino still had said nothing. He stood there, arms folded, lips tight. Lemot's repeated nods encouraging him to speak went unanswered. Duval was giving him no chance anyway.

"Do I understand you?" he shouted. "Joining this guild permits him to stay on in Paris?" He glared at them belligerently. "No, gentlemen. I'm sorry. That won't do. I simply won't accept it."

For a moment all was silence. Massat frowned. He seemed as disturbed as anyone.

"For heaven's sake, Monsieur," he wanted to know, "why take that line? What harm in his staying if David approves his subjects?"

Duval took his stand in the middle of the room, looking first at one, then at another.

"Because, gentlemen, the plan won't work. Because it's plain, gentlemen, you don't know your friend. He may make this promise, he may even make it in good faith, but he'll go right on painting whatever he has in mind to paint, no matter what he's promised, no matter what he's sworn. He'll go right on with these atrocious scenes, those intolerable caricatures. The plain fact, Messieurs, is that our friend here is a compulsive artist. He'll never change, he's quite incapable of changing. And I'm not about to accept his being given another chance to get away with it. I can't and I won't, not for my sake only but for yours too and for all the rest of us, all the people of this country."

"What is this!" Lemot's voice was emotion-choked. "You know what it'll mean if Fouché gets into this. What's got into you? I can't believe, Monsieur, you're that kind of man!"

Duval took a very superior air. "I thought I'd made that plain, Messieurs. I'm not a brute, nor given to hate. I didn't come here to do him harm. I'm here as his friend, to save him, not only from Fouché but from himself. Monsieur Lebrun is about to leave the country. Tonight he'll be leaving for Switzerland. Here is his passport, signed and stamped. Here are a thousand francs to see him on his way. In Switzerland he'll be free to paint anything he likes, anything to which his inspiration moves him."

He held out a purse and the passport toward Topino, who, instead of taking them, came at him so abruptly he was forced back a step.

"Switzerland! You swine! That's what you've had up your sleeve! But don't think you've got me. You may be a genius at swindling the army, but you're poor at judging a man and how far you can push him."

"Young man"—Duval was glaring at him—"the choice isn't yours. It's Switzerland or—"

"Or what? You heard. I've been accepted by the guild. I'm under the protection of the state."

"Are you now?" Head down, Duval was like a bull ready to charge; he was hissing his words. "I take it you've been able to answer all the questions the police asked, but I can think of one they haven't touched on yet—the gunsmith and the package a certain person got from him. It just so happens I know who that person was and I have three witnesses in my household to back me. Don't be upset, though." He paused to see how his words affected the rest of them. "It's entirely up to you whether I open my mouth or not. There's no need for me to say anything unless *you*, Monsieur Lebrun, force me to speak. Again, I have here your passport and—"

Before he could finish, the door was thrown open. Standing there was an officer of the gendarmes. He had rapped three times, he announced, and gotten no reply.

The man was young, trim, very smart in his new uniform and obviously trying to give himself an air of importance.

"Citoyen Topino-Lebrun?" His eyes went around the circle, and when Topino nodded, "May I ask you, *Citoyen,* your whereabouts on the night of October 10th?"

"May I ask by what right you burst into my quarters and . . ."

Lemot cut him off. "You must excuse my friend," he said. "I can tell you what you want to know. *Citoyen* Lebrun never left his room here that entire evening. I can testify to that myself and I can get you other proof if you think you need it."

"Thank you very much, *Citoyen,"* The officer made Lemot an ironic little bow. "But what I really came for is to ask if *Citoyen* Lebrun can help us identify the person who picked up the guns that were found on Arena. We've been given to understand *Citoyen* Lebrun can tell us a good deal about that."

"No, no," Lemot came back instantly. "How could Lebrun know anything about that. He's a painter. He's not interested in guns, he's not interested in politics or even much in France. In fact, he's about to go abroad."

"That was kind of you, François." Topino smiled. "Thank you. But you're mistaken. I'm not going abroad. I'm not about to ask for any favors either except"—he nodded in the direction of Duval—"except on the part of *Citoyen* Duval, who can please me much by relieving us of his execrable presence."

You could see Duval flinch. Other than that he contained himself, and as he turned to Topino only the eyes showed what was going on inside him.

"Monsieur. I believe I told you. I have three witnesses ready to identify the person who picked up this package the police are so eager to know about. It was raining hard that day, but we were all there, on guard you might say. We were glad we could do something to protect the nation from a few *illuminés* set on bringing back the blessings of the Revolution."

"Then you know the person, *Citoyen?*" the officer said. "Be pleased to give me the name."

"All right." Topino turned to the officer. "Enough of that. I can make it quite simple for you." He went across to his easel, and while the others waited for what he would say he

[154]

stood there as if in thought, as if he'd forgotten his visitors and was studying the canvas, seeing a world behind it, flags and storming crowds, walls that crumbled and soldiers fleeing. Then finally, looking up, his eyes still wide, he faced the company and spoke.

"It was I who picked up the guns, I who delivered them to men brave enough to fight for liberty, true enough to give their lives to rid the country of a tyrant."

"Don't listen to him!" Lemot was shouting. "It's all a lie. Duval says he knows the person. Ask him. Question his witnesses!"

"Yes. I do know the person." Duval steadied his voice and looked Topino in the eye. "It was *you.* You were at the gunsmith's. With your permission that's how I'm going to testify."

From Topino there was no answer. The officer laid a hand on his shoulder.

"*Citoyen* Topino-Lebrun"—he raised his voice—"I arrest you on the charge of collaborating with Arena and Ceracchi in the attempt on the life of the First Consul, October 10th at the Theatre des Arts."

Lemot caught Topino's arm.

"For God's sake, deny it. Deny it! Think of your art! Think of the tribunal that will judge you!"

"I never have stopped thinking of it, François."

The officer turned Topino toward the door. "You will come with me."

Before they could move, Massat stepped forward, put his hat on his head, and then, removing it, bowed with a flourish straight out of times gone by.

"*Mes compliments,* Monsieur. I am proud to have known you."

Lemot followed Topino as far as the door and there held him a second.

"I see it all very well now, everything you were trying to tell me. Good-bye, old friend."

On January 10th, 1801, by order of Napoleon Bonaparte, First Consul, Topino-Lebrun, Arena, Ceracchi, and their fellow conspirators died under the guillotine on the Place de Grève, Paris.